"Do You Always Go Swimming Wearing Only A Cowboy Hat?"

Gabe asked curiously.

"That's none of your business," Sara retorted hotly.

"Don't look so flustered. Many women enjoy swimming *au naturel*, and I find it charming." He grinned. "Most prefer bathing caps to Stetsons, though."

Sara colored a pale rose. "If you'll excuse me, I'm going to get dressed—"

"Oh, not on my account, I hope? Please, Miss Tracey, make yourself comfortable—take off the towel and sunbathe if you wish, I don't mind. But just a touch of sun, though, I imagine you burn easily with all that white, white skin."

ASHLEY SUMMERS
lives in Spring, Texas where she keeps a "ten room house, a fat Schnauzer, a grouchy cat, and, occasionally, a grandson." She has several writing projects underway and the most important influence on her work is her "fantastic husband."

Dear Reader:

Silhouette has always tried to give you exactly what you want. When you asked for increased realism, deeper characterization and greater length, we brought you Silhouette Special Editions. When you asked for increased sensuality, we brought you Silhouette Desire. Now you ask for books with the length and depth of Special Editions, the sensuality of Desire, but with something else besides, something that no one else offers. Now we bring you SILHOUETTE INTIMATE MOMENTS, true romance novels, longer than the usual, with all the depth that length requires. More sensuous than the usual, with characters whose maturity matches that sensuality. Books with the ingredient no one else has tapped: excitement.

There is an electricity between two people in love that makes everything they do magic, larger than life—and this is what we bring you in SILHOUETTE INTIMATE MOMENTS. Look for them this May, wherever you buy books.

These books are for the woman who wants more than she has ever had before. These books are for you. As always, we look forward to your comments and suggestions. You can write to me at the address below:

Karen Solem
Editor-in-Chief
Silhouette Books
P.O. Box 769
New York, N.Y. 10019

ASHLEY SUMMERS
A Private Eden

Silhouette Romance

Published by Silhouette Books New York

America's Publisher of Contemporary Romance

Other Silhouette Books by Ashley Summers

Fires of Memory
Season of Enchantment

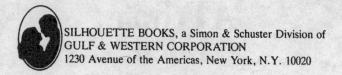

SILHOUETTE BOOKS, a Simon & Schuster Division of
GULF & WESTERN CORPORATION
1230 Avenue of the Americas, New York, N.Y. 10020

ISBN: 0-671-57223-7

First Silhouette Books printing May, 1983

10 9 8 7 6 5 4 3 2 1

Map by Ray Lundgren

America's Publisher of Contemporary Romance

Printed in the U.S.A.

To Lawrence, who knows why

A Private Eden

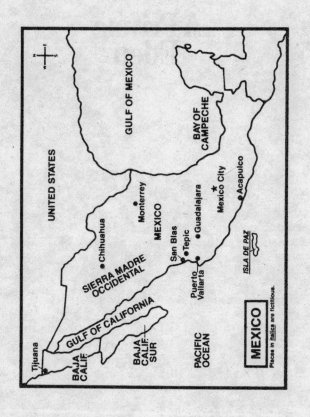

MEXICO

Places in _italics_ are fictitious.

Chapter One

Sara seldom lost her temper, but when she broke a fingernail opening the firmly sealed box, an explosive curse split the air, and a hot rush of tears spilled down her cheeks. She felt like kicking the blasted thing! Hearing the foyer door slam, she raced to the small bathroom and hurriedly washed her face. She had intended to leave early precisely for this reason; she'd been perilously near tears all afternoon, and a kind word from anyone—particularly her employer—would serve to crack the dam. But the box of books had arrived just as she was putting on her coat, and she felt obliged to unpack it—this hidebound conscience of hers!

Adjusting the collar of her gray wool dress, she gave herself a hasty check and decided she would pass muster. She saw no point in upsetting Alex with her distress, and by the time he entered the office, she was determined to be her usual composed self, even if she had to bite her tongue!

Alex passed the office door with a jaunty wave and went into his study. Relieved at this brief respite, Sara sat down at her desk and picked up the glossy-jacketed novel. She had typed every page in this book at least three times, and she could still lose herself in its fascinating contents, which was why Alex Brandt's novels were consistently on the best seller lists, she thought warmly; they were as addictive as hot buttered popcorn! She had worked for the noted author for three years, and was his number one fan.

"Had and was; past tense," she whispered sadly. Tears clogged her throat again. Sara closed the book and put it aside, wiping her cheeks like a child. For all practical purposes, she was now unemployed. That morning Alex had informed her that he was closing the apartment and leaving New York for an indefinite time. Even with an entire day to absorb the shock, she still experienced the same jolt of hurt each time she consciously thought of it. After two years of being a mere number in a secretarial pool, the position of private secretary to Alex Brandt had been an exhilarating challenge. One she'd fulfilled well enough to do her honor, she thought with a proud lift of chin.

Over the years Sara had gradually begun taking care of him; besides routine clerical work and shielding him from any preventable unpleasantness and infringements upon his time, she did everything from see to his cleaning and laundry services to ordering his groceries and supervising his parties. After giving so much, it was a rude shock to realize he could get along very well without her. She had certainly over estimated her value, thought Sara wryly.

Well, Alex had promised her excellent references,

and she would have no trouble securing another position, one just as interesting, perhaps even as glamorous, she assured herself. The more she tried to bolster her spirits, though, the more depressed she got—and these aggravating tears! She was not an emotional person, but she was very fond of Alex Brandt.

The wind beating against the window had a raw, scratchy sound. Sara shivered. She felt cold and lonely and hurt, feelings she concealed from Alex's troubled brown eyes as he entered the office. Smiling at the chubby little man, she stood up with unconscious deference. "Good evening, Mr. Brandt. I was just leaving—unless there's something pressing?"

Alex walked to the window and roughly drew the drapes against the gathering night. "This irascible weather!" he exclaimed, looking as irascible as the weather.

"Yes, irascible," Sara wryly agreed. "Would you like that box unpacked tonight, or can it wait?"

"Oh, it can wait. Sara, it occurred to me that you're free to travel, nothing holding you here since . . ."

"Since my father died," Sara finished smoothly. "Yes, I'm quite free, and more than willing to travel. What did you have in mind?" she asked over the sudden leap of her heart. Her throat constricted as he gave her his boyishly abashed grin, guaranteed to make a woman yearn to pat his curly head.

Alex perched on the edge of her desk. "What I had in mind was keeping a secretary I've become genuinely fond of and who takes my sometimes unpleasant disposition in stride," he said gruffly. "What would you say to a house on a private island off the coast of Mexico, with stables for riding and the ocean for swimming and orchids for the picking? A place where the sun shines three hundred and sixty days a year, give or take a day.

There are only thirty houses on the entire island, all privately owned and randomly occupied, since they're mostly vacation homes . . ."

He grinned at her astounded face. "Now, suppose we go there for a few months and see if I can jolt this brain of mine back on the track. Would you be willing to consider it?"

Sara released her breath in a long sigh and searched for her voice. When she found it, it was awfully near a croak. "Alex, I think you're more than just irascible, I think you've gone mad! You offer me a fabulous island with sunshine and beaches and orchids for the picking —and you ask if I'd be *willing* to *consider* it?"

He grinned. "Can I take that as agreement?"

"I most definitely do agree!"

"Careful, Sara, you're getting excited," he solemnly warned.

Sara blushed. She wore chic, tailored clothes, a sleek chignon and what she hoped was an air of sophistication, and her habit of blushing was an intense aggravation. Looking even more flustered on top of another blush, she sat down and crossed her fashionably booted legs.

"When do we leave? I only have to notify my roommate and pack a bag," she said, ignoring his teasing grin.

"Well, I've just found out I have to stay in New York until the end of the month, but I have an idea. Why don't you go on ahead and open the house and engage servants. Would you mind two weeks alone?"

"Bliss," she said simply. "You don't know my roommate. She's a love, but she does love to talk," she added at his puzzled look. "Is this house yours? And a private island—I can't imagine owning an *island!*"

"The house belongs to my sister. The island itself is a sort of corporate thing, largely owned by the Fielding family, but they've sold small shares to a privileged few. I've only been there once, but it seemed a simple life—the kind it takes a couple million bucks to create," Alex said with cheerful envy.

"These Fieldings—what are they like?" Sara eagerly inquired.

"I've never actually met any of them, but they're Texans, rich as sin, of course. The son more or less manages the island."

"The son? How old is he?"

Alex frowned. "I have no idea. But since he's the head of a very large Texas firm, I'd assume he's about my age."

"In other words, tall, dark and handsome," Sara assured.

"Short, bald and paunchy is more like it," Alex sourly corrected. "But he's bound to be a wise man—if I remember correctly, he's never been married."

Sara chuckled. Alex's alimony check was on her desk, waiting for his signature. "I personally find it exceedingly odd that a man could reach your age and not have been married at least once," she consoled.

"I find it exceedingly smart, myself," Alex sighed. His cheeky grin flashed again. "It's all settled then?"

"It's settled—if you're sure you won't need me those two weeks?"

"Naw, I've got private affairs to attend to." He looked at her shrewdly. "Besides, how long has it been since you've had a vacation, hum?"

Sara blushed, wondering if he knew she worked the two weeks he gave her each year. "I don't remember—when I was about twelve, I think," she laughed. Her face worked. "Oh, Mr. Brandt, I—how can I say thank you?" she asked, desperately fighting tears.

"Ha, better wait on the thank you. We'll be working, you know," Alex replied, looking stern. His face softened. "Sara, lest you be concerned about impropriety, we will be properly chaperoned, and it is not considered unusual for a businessman to bring along a member of his staff. No raised eyebrows, my dear," he assured.

Sara concealed a smile. "I don't give a fig for raised eyebrows, Mr. Brandt, and I certainly had no such concern," she softly declared. Alex was forty-eight, and as befitted his age and profession, a fashionably cynical man, yet he was old-fashioned and gallant in many ways, particularly where she was concerned. He might unleash his frustrations on her now and then and pinken her cheeks with lusty curses, but he treated her with utmost respect; strictly business, she thought gladly.

"No boyfriend to resent your leaving?" he asked with a teasing grin.

"Not even one that will know I've left," she replied.

Sara had to hold her hands to keep from giving him the affectionate hug she needed. That she had not lost her job after all, but was now offered this dazzling prospect, threatened to overwhelm her for a moment. It really was hard not to get excited, she gravely admitted to herself.

Her shining blue eyes raised to meet his. "Okay, Mr. Brandt, I'll go on ahead. With all due speed," she added, shivering at the slash of sleet against the window.

"Sara, it will mean Christmas alone," Alex reminded.

"Oh, I'm used to that—no problem," she assured. "Oh heavens, I nearly forgot, there was an urgent call from your agent . . ." Sara picked up her pad and tore off a sheet. "Urgent," she prodded as Alex studied it.

"All calls from my agent are urgent," he sighed.

"And if you'll sign this check now, I'll get it in the morning mail," she suggested.

"I knew I should have stayed at the club and had another martini," Alex glumly informed the telephone.

When she finally left the office at the rear of his apartment and stepped out into the wet December night, Sara wrapped her coat more tightly around her and cheerfully headed for the subway. New York shimmered with Christmas, and it was impossible not to smile at the world. A good forty minutes later, she crunched up the icy steps and opened the door of an apartment which was a far cry from the Ritz. Groping for the lightswitch, she snapped it on and set her purse on the table which was already overflowing with newspapers and fashion sketches. Her roommate Billie was not the neatest person.

But she was a lovely one, Sara quickly defended against her irritation at the messy apartment. During the two years when Sara's father had lain paralyzed in a nursing home, Billie had been a compassionate, supportive friend, and—more times than Sara liked to remember—had come up with the rent when she didn't have her share. Billie was sophisticated and experienced, a fashion model of some note with a marvelously flippant attitude about life and men. She was Sara's complete opposite, yet they were the best of friends.

Disappointed that the bubbly blond was not there to share her fabulous news, Sara hung up her coat and briskly rubbed her shoulders. The apartment was dank and chilly. With little hope of affecting a change, she turned up the thermostat, then went to the tiny closet of a kitchen to put the kettle on.

A few minutes later, the door flew open, and a fur-wrapped creature blew in on a gust of bitterly cold wind. "Oh, Billie, thank heavens you've come home—I have something wonderful to tell you!" Sara cried. "Come, take off your coat, I'm making hot chocolate—"

"Oh, honey, I haven't time for chocolate. I've got a date and only twenty minutes to get ready," Billie replied. "But what's your news? Come tell me while I'm dressing, okay?"

"Okay. Oh, Billie, it's the most fantastic thing—nothing like this has ever happened to me before!"

"You've met a man!" Billie squealed. "Marvelous! I knew you would someday. What's he look like? What does he do, is he rich, does he—"

"Bil-lie! Will you just hush up and listen? I have not met a man!" came Sara's exasperated shout. Billie looked terribly pained, but she hushed, and Sara raked half a dozen garments off one of the twin beds, then sat down and excitedly told her the news.

Billie's reaction was all she could want and then some. Delightedly Sara watched her friend go off like a skyrocket, flinging sparkling questions in every direction. Some twenty-five minutes later they remembered her date, and Sara guiltily helped her dress.

"Billie, remember, if you can't find someone to share the apartment for a few months, I'll still send my part of the rent," Sara assured, following her to the door.

Listening to the sleet slashing the window, she aired her opinion that a person would have to be mad to go out in that frigid hell just to meet a man. Billie looked pained again. That Sara had reached the ancient age of twenty-four without getting seriously involved with a man absolutely horrified Billie. While everyone else was out there writhing in the delicious throes of passion or broken hearts or beginning affairs which looked ripe with promise, Sara just shook her head in bemused wonder and went her quiet, unruffled way. That seemed peculiar to Billie, and several times she had suggested professional therapy for this dreadful affliction.

After her friend went on her merry way, Sara sat down at the table with a cup of lukewarm chocolate. Maybe there really was something wrong with her, she mused in idle concern. She was attractive, and her air of cool indifference served to intrigue masculine interest, but nothing ever came of it. Billie declared Sara's marked aversion to what Sara termed the dinner-theater-nightcap-bed date to be a disaster when it came to building relationships.

Was she peculiar? Perhaps even freaky, as Billie so often accused? Was crawling into some man's bed a requisite to maturity? Right offhand she couldn't think of any beds she wanted to crawl into. Besides, Billie was either constantly entangled in love's sweet agony, or bitterly bemoaning the lack of it, which seemed to Sara a most unsettling state of mind!

Perhaps it was odd that no man had even so much as got her flustered, Sara reflected, but she really didn't think she needed therapy. Sooner or later, she supposed she'd meet someone and feel something, love or passion or whatever they called it, and marriage and children would follow as naturally as spring followed winter. No need to get into a stew about it, she concluded comfortably. She washed out the teacup and went into the bedroom. As usual, it was a wild clutter of undergarments and discarded dresses strewn about by Billie in her quest for the perfect outfit. Sara automatically put away and hung up until she'd achieved order. If anyone needed a rich husband, Billie did, she thought, chuckling. She'd require a maid whose sole function in life was to follow her about picking up clothes!

Shedding her dress for a flannel nightgown and wool socks, Sara got between the icy sheets and pulled the quilt over her head, then gave herself up to utterly delicious thoughts. Day after tomorrow she would leave this snowbound city and then—two weeks alone on a sundrenched island, with servants and unimaginable luxuries! The Fieldings were a Texas family, Alex said, decades of wealth and position. She had never associated with those kind of people—would she fit in?

"You're a secretary, you nitwit, not a member of the club," she scolded her romping imagination. But Alex said informality was the rule, and that he had found everyone friendly. Of course, Alex Brandt could go anywhere and find everyone friendly! It didn't matter whether or not she fit in; sunshine and water and golden beaches—*bliss!*

Back in what Sara termed the golden years, when she had lived with her parents in a neat brownstone near Gramercy Park, there had been money for ballet, piano and riding lessons. Ballet had proved to be a waste, but she still retained her musical skills, and a rusty sort of riding ability. Very rusty. The beautiful palomino mare she rode now was skittish and tender-mouthed, a thoroughbred who knew her rider was less than an expert, and was naturally nervous about that.

"Easy, Alana, easy, girl," Sara soothed, patting the golden neck. She guided the horse down a gentle incline, keeping to the ill-defined path, since a week of exploring the island had not yet familiarized her with its terrain. She had imagined it would be small and rigidly structured; instead Isla de Paz was impressive hills and deep green valleys alive with brilliantly colored birds. There were no orchids that she could see, but other gorgeous flowers abounded, many of them familiar, and there were majestic palms and white sand beaches if one tired of subtropical forests or manicured grasslands.

The rugged windward side of the island was an official bird sanctuary, the leeward side given to large, gleaming white houses, each an estate in itself, set in lush green lawns behind gorgeously flowered poinsettia or hibiscus hedges, overlooking a placid turquoise bay. There was a nine-hole golf course, a small airstrip, and an impressive marina from which a sleek white ferry plied to and from the mainland. Other than a handsome club which contained a small bar and restaurant, and a grocery store offering such basic necessities as fresh milk and tinned caviar, the island had no defiling businesses of any sort.

Verdant and fruitful, Isla de Paz served no practical purpose that Sara could see. It seemed to exist solely for the pleasure of a few wealthy families.

Engaging the servants—a maid named Elena and a part-time gardener—and getting settled in had taken all of a day. From then on Sara was left on her glorious own. Although she received friendly waves now and then, no one disturbed her or made overtures of any kind. Since she felt shy around the people she saw gathering on the clubhouse veranda each evening, she kept to herself, figuring there would be plenty of time, when Alex arrived, to properly meet the residents.

Meanwhile, she had discovered the stables and, thus, rekindled an old pleasure. When she had introduced herself to Skeet, the stable manager, she was given one of the Fielding horses to ride whenever she desired, which was nearly every day. After all, there was a lot of beautiful territory to explore, and a horse provided the means to do it.

Like practically everything else on the island, the stables belonged to the Fieldings. Judging from the scant facts Alex had given her, it was the son's private playground, Sara derisively concluded. Her peripheral brushes with wealth, gained through Alex's vast circle of friends and acquaintances, had left a bad taste in her mouth. Despite her seeming maturity, Sara was essentially an innocent, and being propositioned by a man whose wife was standing less than ten feet away did not strike her as amusing, yet it had happened on several occasions—nasty incidents she had kept secret from Alex.

The few times she had played hostess for his parties, the speculative and even downright insinuating male looks directed at them were mortifying to her. She considered Alex to be one of the kindest, most decent people she had ever met, and was hotly chagrined that anyone would defile their relationship with salacious thoughts.

She had met men like Robert Fielding before, she thought scornfully—men who thought their wealth entitled them to any woman they fancied! Of course, he might actually be a decent sort, but all the evidence pointed to the contrary—rich, middle-aged and never been married? That was suspect in anybody's book! Since he kept a house there, she supposed she would eventually meet the man, but she had no real desire to do so. And, she admitted, the thought of meeting him was a little intimidating. What a formidable person he must be! Owning an island probably made him some sort of king, at least in his estimation.

No time for woolgathering, Sara, she scolded herself as the mare shied sideways. A cloud of pale yellow butterflies suddenly lifted, like a low-lying mist, and fluttered ahead, then settled again on a bush with the same concerted movement. Reining in, Sara gave a pleased cry as she looked around her. The tiny stream she had abstractedly followed gave over to a series of shallow black stone ledges, below which a deep green pool spread out in an oblong circle. It looked so inviting, she was greatly tempted, but she had nothing to bathe in.

Pushing back the cream-colored Stetson which had been Billie's frivolous going away gift, Sara considered her wicked urge. Other than the contentedly browsing mare, she was alone. And hot and sweaty. She looked again at the pool under its canopy of leaves. It was an idyllic scene, soft and enticing, complete with the siren song of tumbling waters. And she did have a towel with her. This item, as well as her trusty thermos of limeade, made for a pleasant pause in her rides when she spread the towel in some lovely glen and lay upon it sipping the cool drink, even napping in the warm afternoon sunlight. . . .

A short time later, she had stripped off her clothes and was heading for the pool, her naked body gleaming in the greenish sunlight. The cowboy hat still sat on her head. She had crammed her hair under it, and was using it as a unique sort of bathing cap.

Opening the small satchel, she extracted the pink velour towel. As she spread it on the bank, she gave a swift, guarded look around her. What would Billie think of prim little Sara now, skinny-dipping in a woodland pool! The thought was delightful, and she gingerly pushed through the ferns which fringed the pool and stepped into the shallow water.

To her surprise, the bottom was more sand than muck, and it deepened rapidly; after half a dozen steps, she was hip deep. Carefully she moved deeper until the water covered her shoulders, then relaxed letting herself drift, keeping one foot touching bottom so as not to endanger her precious hat. Marvelous! She felt like a Lorelei, all silky skin and lissome body. Next time, though, she would bring a proper bathing cap, since trying to keep the Stetson dry was a bother. Dreamily adrift with pleasant thoughts, she closed her eyes and floated in the caressingly cool water while time passed as effortlessly as breathing.

From the corner of her eye, Sara suddenly caught a movement in the water near a clump of willows, and all pleasant thoughts were abruptly driven from her mind! The jolting shock of fear was so sudden, she screamed shrilly. She had only a blurred impression of the thing, but it was long and ugly and possibly dangerous, and she began floundering through the water with only one objective in mind: to reach shore and give over the pool to whatever that thing was!

Stumbling and falling, she hit the shallows and practically crawled up the bank in her haste to escape it—whatever *it* was! She had seen no menacing creatures in her forays through the island—was it a crocodile? Surely someone would have warned her if they had crocodiles here! It was too small for a crocodile, wasn't it? But crocodiles started out small, she reminded herself, and if it was one, it had parents!

Scrambling through the ferns, Sara snatched up the towel and wrapped it around her from breasts to mid-thigh. Any sort of wild creature was beyond her experience, and her heart was pounding both from her exertions, and her fright. As she anxiously searched the surface of the pool for whatever lurked there, it occurred to her that crocodiles were also well adapted to land. Clutching her towel at this dreadful thought, she began walking backwards with prudent speed.

A twig snapped sharply behind her. Sara turned with a startled scream, and for an instant, the huge golden stallion and its tall rider silhouetted against the sun were as frightening as her imagined crocodile!

Chapter Two

Sara's heart jumped so violently, she nearly dropped her towel! It was a toss-up as to which was more alarming, the thing in the water, or the man who slid off his horse and started towards her. A splashing sound behind her decided the issue. Giving a shrill little scream, Sara grabbed hold of her cowboy hat with one hand and her towel with the other, and scrambled up the slippery slope in wild-eyed haste.

"What's the matter!" he exclaimed as she flung herself at him.

"Something . . . in the water—I think it was a crocodile!" she gasped.

Cradling her gently in his arms, he searched the pool for a moment, then burst out laughing. "There's your crocodile," he said, pointing to the scaly green monstrosity scudding up the opposite bank. "That's an iguana. We don't have crocodiles here."

Sara's blush ran from the top of her head to the tips

of her curling toes. "An iguana?" she echoed tremulously.

"Um hum. Iguanas rarely eat people, even half naked ones," he blandly assured.

"Well, I didn't get a good look at the thing, I was too busy getting away from it! And they don't have iguanas running around New York, you know—you stop that laughing this minute!" Sara ordered furiously.

As another burst of rich, husky laughter obeyed her command, Sara thought she had never felt so mortified in her life! He had a beautifully shaped mouth and perfect teeth and he was easily ten feet tall. She scowled ferociously. Who was he, one of the stablehands? Probably so, she thought, eyeing his shabby jeans, and a rude one at that!

"I am delighted this amuses you," she said icily. His eyes were a gold-flecked green, fringed with thick, dark lashes—the kind women paid dearly for. Realizing those eyes were roaming over her with lusty interest, Sara cringed as a welter of sensations crowded in. His hands felt warm on her naked back and were moving cozily downwards. With his face only inches away, Sara's pulse raced in startled response to his clean, masculine smell, and she felt a sweet heated coil of excitement at the brush of his thighs.

She looked up at him and her hat fell off. He laughed in open delight as a rain of soft black curls spilled down her neck. She was on fire with embarrassment, it sweeping through her cheeks and flashing from her hot blue eyes. Her mind swarming with outraged words, Sara opened her mouth to cut down this infuriating male.

"Oh!" she stated.

"Wonderful, just wonderful," he murmured, catching up a handful of her hair.

"Oh!" she said incredulously.

"Say it again and I'm going to kiss it." A flash of white teeth accompanied his insouciant warning. Feeling caught in a whirlpool, she stared at him while she frantically sought to collect her wits. Another indignant gasp parted her lips. He kissed them.

Sara's eyes widened with shock as his mouth set on hers. His arms curved around her like steel bands—and the hands yet clutching her towel—pinned against his chest. Shock gave way to anger, but her wild twisting only served to drive her softness into the unyielding male body. His mouth pressed warm and hard, demanding a response she had absolutely no intention of giving. She stopped struggling and stood stiffly, repulsed by his insolence.

He raised his head a fraction, his eyes gleaming at her denial. He laughed, low and husky, and then his mouth settled onto hers in a deep, sensual, gathering-in kiss that was like no other she had known.

Sara struggled, and then stopped as a strange, flaring delight invaded her body. Warm and firm, his mouth explored hers, forcing her lips open for the sensual probe of his tongue, arousing a swift, primitive need in her to respond to this demanding male. When she made a little sound of protest, his arms tightened and pressed her intimately against his hard, lean frame while his mouth teased and delighted her senses.

It was timeless, without beginning or end, this sweet, firey play of lips and tongues. Sara was dimly aware of the hands moving down her back, his fingers burning through the towel, holding her urgently close until she sagged in his arms. Had her hands not been trapped between them, they would have lost themselves in his dark, glossy hair; as it was, her body melted into his, her lips soft and clinging, inviting this outrageous plunder.

When he abruptly released her, Sara staggered backwards, feeling dazed and weak, and then ablaze with fury at him and at herself! She was weak and trembling and how dare he make her feel this way!

"How *dare* you!" she hissed in chaotic fury. The sardonic gleam of amusement in his eyes gave her pause. He was obviously anticipating the slap in the face she was on the very brink of delivering! Snatching back her hand, she flushed scarlet at her predictable behavior. She was Sara Tracey, who could command respect from a New York cab driver with her haughty manner, she reminded herself rather desperately. She hitched her towel up higher and sought to put this situation in its proper perspective, but just what the perspective was kept eluding her.

"Now you see here!" she began furiously, but all sorts of things were scampering through her mind. Good grief, he might be an escaped convict, a rapist, a madman, she thought. He didn't look alarming, though. He simply looked warm and friendly and heart-catchingly male. And deliciously amused. She glared at him. He laughed and touched her nose. She had a wild thought about getting dressed, but just how to manage that without inciting his interest had not yet resolved itself.

Haughtily clutching her towel, she raised her pretty nose in the air and asked, "Who are you? Are you one of the stable hands?"

He grinned. "Um, I guess you could say that. You have the loveliest eyes I've ever seen, one minute soft and innocent as dawn, the next, fire and lightning challenge—"

"I'm really not interested in your opinion of my eyes," Sara snapped. "Do you work here or not?"

He grinned again, but other than a noncommittal shrug, her question went unanswered. Sara nibbled her lip as she studied the rugged set of his features. He had thick, unruly hair as glossy as sable, and he was powerfully built—slim and tall with a tigerish grace in every long line of that handsome male body. Wasn't he a little bit too old to be a hand? Most of the workers she had seen around the island were in their teens or early twenties, bronzed young men who kept aloof from the residents, and this one was at least thirty, and certainly not aloof!

He smiled at her just then, and her conviction wavered. That air of self-assurance had an odd arrogance about it. He looked like someone who not only knew exactly what he wanted, but was supremely confident of getting it!

His slanting eyebrow suggested that her silence was overlong. Sara flushed hotly and checked the folds of her towel in a manner which proclaimed it perfectly natural to be standing there wearing a towel. After all, she was much more fully covered than when she wore her bikini—and thank heavens she didn't have on that tiny thing!

"Are you employed by the stables?" she asked coldly. "I would like your name, please. I fully intend to report you—" That arrogant grin again! "I'm quite certain they don't approve of female guests being assaulted," she stiffly announced.

His eyes widened with astonishment. "Assaulted? I merely kissed you, that's hardly assault. Besides, it could be argued that I had reason—ample provocation, in fact. Didn't you enjoy it?"

"I certainly did not!"

Cynical green eyes roamed down her until she felt stripped of even the towel. "Now how could I have been so mistaken? I could have sworn I held a willing woman in my arms."

"Well, you didn't," Sara said flatly. "The only thing you held was a woman who endured your disgusting kiss because you're physically stronger than she is!" Listening to her scathing tone, Sara was satisfied that it would scotch even the most uncivilized male.

"You endured it, hum?" he murmured, looking not at all scotched.

"I had no choice, did I?" she coldly returned.

"Um, I suppose not, since I wanted it and I usually get what I want."

"Do you?" Sara's lip curled as she coolly examined him. He was so attractive that he unsettled a woman with just a glance from those sexy green eyes. And didn't he know it! "Mr.— X, at the risk of sounding repetitious, could we dispense with your egomania and get on with the matter at hand, which is, what is your name? I think even you'll agree that I've been exceedingly patient, but there is a limit," she said, keeping it stern and reasonable.

He looked down at her heaving bosom. "Beautiful," he sighed. His lazy green eyes got all tangled up with hers again. "You display something as tempting as this and you actually expect me to keep my hands off?" he asked with outrageous astonishment.

"I—you—really!" Sara choked. Realizing this was scarcely a daunting reply, she stuck out her chin and blazed, "When it's not yours to touch, yes, I expect you to keep your hands off!"

"Ah, that's the problem. I didn't realize it wasn't mine to touch," he said with the delighted air of discovery. "No wedding ring, you see."

Sara gaped. "If there's no wedding ring, you think that—that it's—"

"Available," he confirmed. His grin flashed. "Or at the least, touchable."

"I am neither available nor touchable—"

"Most delectably touchable," he murmured.

"Nor am I flattered that you think so!" she plowed on. His smile knowingly denied this, and she simply *had* to put down that maddening male arrogance! Just then he casually twined a finger through a silky black curl, his manner so insouciant, Sara felt unhinged. "Stop that—keep your hands off me! Just who do you think you are, a second-rate Robert Fielding?" she cried wildly, the name coming from out of nowhere like a blazing symbol of contempt.

Green eyes narrowed. "What do you know of Robert Fielding?"

Even more rattled at his sharp demand, Sara sputtered, "Well, I—I don't know anything about the man himself. I was speaking categorically, of a—a certain type of man," she defied his quizzical regard.

"Without even meeting the man, you know his type? Clairvoyant, perhaps," he suggested.

How in the world had she gotten into this! Even more importantly, how would she get out of it with any dignity at all? And did he have to look so *judicial?* "I only meant—well, he's rich, single, amoral—sort of a prototype of the men I've met," she floundered. Why didn't he say something and get her off the hook! "The sort of man who thinks women are here for the specific purpose of—for his pleasure, that he can grab at anything that catches his fancy just because . . . he wants to," she ran down.

"You know all that about Robert Fielding and you've never even met him? Amazing!"

"Oh, will you stop it? I don't actually know anything about him, I was speaking broadly! All I meant was that you have a remarkably similar affliction!" she exploded. "You see something you like, you reach out and—and grab it without a second thought!"

"A splendid philosophy, seems to me. After all, how many people do you know right now who are sitting around bemoaning missed opportunities?" he approved, his rakish grin a tickle of excitement racing up her spine.

This had gone far enough, and she refused to stand here and argue with this arrogant male! "I'm certain I don't know," Sara said with massive disdain. "Could we get back to a subject which does interest me, namely, your insolence and the retribution which I fully intend to exact?"

"Do you always go swimming wearing only a cowboy hat?" he asked curiously.

Sara's offense was neatly shot to pieces. "No, I—I had just washed my hair, you see, and I—that's none of your business!"

"Don't look so flustered, Sara, many of the women here enjoy nude bathing and I find it charming," he soothed. "Most prefer bathing caps to Stetsons, though," he added wryly.

Sara managed to grab onto a startled fact as it swam by her. "How do you know my name?"

"Why, you registered at the stables, remember? How do you like Alana?"

"The maid?" she asked, by now too confused to follow.

"No, the mare," he said, glancing at the pretty little mare affectionately nuzzling the big, handsome stallion. "They're very good friends," he leaned near to confide.

31

Sara colored a pale rose. "If you'll excuse me, I'm going to get dressed—"

"Oh, not on my account, I hope? Please, Miss Tracey, make yourself comfortable—take off the towel and sunbathe if you wish, I don't mind. You have lovely legs, by the way. I imagine you burn easily, though, with all that white, white skin," he ended in a caressing murmur.

Insolent green eyes danced all over that white skin which was rapidly becoming a spectacular sunset pink. The cloud of ebony hair tumbling wildly around her shoulders drew his regard before his critical gaze moved back to the creamy curves of her breasts, and the sweetly rounded hips snuggled against the soft pink terry cloth. He examined her trim ankles and coral-tipped toes before his eyes wandered lazily upwards again, to collide with her hyacinth blue eyes. He smiled a slow, curling smile of such utter male arrogance, that Sara felt a maddening urge to slap him. She had never met a man she could not handle with the lethal weapon of feminine scorn. Yet he simply refused to recognize it, and how could she squash a man who didn't realize he was being squashed!

"You are an eminently kissable woman, Miss Tracey," he said huskily. "Who could censure my mad impulse?"

"I am not," she heatedly denied. Her words backed up in her ears at the amusement deepening his eyes. "Could you please give me your name?" she half choked. The pulse throbbing at her throat was a maddening distraction. Try as she would, she could not recapture her composure; every time he grinned, the curved lines in his cheeks chipped away fragments of her control.

Infuriated at her reaction, she stamped her foot, an exceedingly stupid thing to do. "I intend to file a formal complaint, you can be sure of that!" Sara said through gritted teeth, making a hasty recovery of her towel. Her voice rose to a screech. "I'll have you run off this island with a—a horsewhip!"

He gave her a sunny smile. "In that case, you may call me Gabe."

What was the matter with the man, she wondered, completely bewildered at his lack of concern. Her voice steadied, cold and level. "I don't intend to call you anything. Now would you mind if I got dressed?"

"You go right ahead," Gabe permitted.

She took several deep breaths which he watched with interest. "I would prefer privacy, Mr.— Gabe!" Something exploded in her head as he retrieved the Stetson and set it on her curls, and then had the cheek to smooth them from her face. For a horrified instant, she thought he was going to kiss her again, and then she wished that he would. She turned flaming red at her incorrigible thought.

Gabe watched her with an air of indulgent amusement. "Just Gabe will be fine. Oh, do go ahead with your dressing, I'll just watch the pool and stay alert for crocodiles. Ferocious beasts, I hear, that eat a woman in one quick bite," he warned darkly. "Mr. Fielding is highly protective of his female guests; he's likely to get incensed should one of them get eaten." Cutting a glance at Sara's crimson face, he walked to the mare and fondled her nose. "How you doing, girl, hum? You enjoy riding Miss Tracey? Looks to have a fine seat, doesn't she!"

Sara broke into a run at his last words. She was a small, slim woman who had at various times been described as cute or pretty or even lovely, but never as eminently kissable, or even as having a fine seat. The deep chuckle tingling her ears increased her speed. Snatching up her clothes, she ducked into a tangle of shrubbery and put on her underwear with aggravating clumsiness. Her body was damp, and the thin nylon panties clung to her hips in uncooperative rolls. Furiously she yanked at them, then reached for her jeans. There was a black beetle caught in the hem. Her muffled voice carried clearly.

"Need any help, Miss Tracey?" Gabe called in a killingly unctuous voice.

Where did that beetle go! "No, thank you," she called. A fingernail snapped on the obstinate jeans—what on earth had happened to the woman who could chop down a man with a look! "Sure isn't around here now," she muttered angrily. The black-and-white checkered shirt had impossibly tiny buttons, but she fastened enough to conceal her bra. She then raked her fingers through her hair and crammed the tangled mess under her hat. Giving a last tug at her tight jeans, Sara calmly strolled out of concealment.

He was still there, leaning lazily against a tree and smiling that utterly maddening smile. She had never met such a loathsomely confident man, she thought, as his green eyes roamed over her hips.

"I liked you better without clothes," he observed.

She walked rigidly past him to the mare. As she put a foot in the stirrup, a hand on her bottom froze her in midair; a second later she was given a forceful boost into the saddle. "Oh!" she gasped. Clawing at the saddlehorn to avoid sailing over the other side, she gave him a wildly incredulous look. He was utterly *impossible!*

He grinned. "Careful, Sara, you're provoking me again."

"Mr. Gabe, you are the most obnoxious, arrogant, totally *uncivilized* man I have ever met! You stop it—you just stop it!" she warned, outraged at that grin and the twinkling green eyes and, most of all, the inexplicable effect he was having on her nervous system!

Feeling in danger of flying apart, she struck at the hand laying casually on her leg, and dug her heels into the mare's sides. Save for edging closer to the stallion, the animal paid no heed.

"Will you come *on!*" she gritted, yanking at the reins. A hand swooped down on her wrist in a vice-like grip, and she was suddenly looking into flinty green eyes. A different man stood beside her, a tall, forbidding stranger whose easy manner had abruptly given way to a chilling look of anger.

"Alana's got a tender mouth—stop that sawing at the reins!" Gabe commanded. "If you don't know how to treat a horse, then get yourself off her!" His fingers bit deep into her soft flesh. Genuinely alarmed for the first time, Sara caught her breath.

"Please, Gabe, I wasn't mistreating her; I love horses! I just wanted to go and she doesn't," she said weakly.

His hard line of mouth relaxed at her tremulous plea. "Of course you weren't mistreating her. I'm sorry, Sara. But she is a very sensitive animal, remember that. You were given the privilege of riding these horses, don't ever abuse that privilege," he warned with dangerous softness.

Gabe caressed the sleek velvet nose which turned into his hand as he spoke. *"Vaya,* Alana," he said firmly, and gave the mare's rump a light slap. Unprepared for the instant response, Sara was nearly unseated as Alana pranced sideways, then set out for the corral at a fast clip. Gabe's laughter kept pace for a few feet, then was mercifully gone.

Sara's anger returned full force once she had escaped that unsettling presence. "Arrogant, domineering brute!" she muttered viciously. She looked behind several times, but the arrogant wretch hadn't followed her. He probably hadn't dared, she thought, and, well, he should be worried! When she got through with him—!

She rode into the corral in a surge of vindictive spirit. It was late afternoon, and the attractive white structure which housed the horses looked deserted except for the young man who took Alana in hand with soothing little murmurs in liquid-sounding Spanish. Sara looked around with furious intent. Where was the man called Skeet?

"Sēnor Skeet?" she asked, addressing the handsome brown boy.

"Ees gone," he said, shrugging.

Sara's lips thinned. "Very well, I'll speak with him tomorrow. How many hands do you have around here?" The expressive brown eyes shrugged, greatly adding to Sara's frustration. She had seen only two males around the stables besides this one, and none of them were called Gabe.

"Gabe?" she tested.

The boy broke into a wide grin. "Ah, Sēnor Gabe!" he crowed, nodding.

Sara gave it up. At least she definitely knew Gabe was a hand. Actually, she reflected, all she knew was that the boy knew Gabe's name. Just before leaving, she peeked into the stall which held the beautiful palomino stallion, but it was empty. Maybe Gabe had decided to take a swim and then drowned.

The house was still and cool, and mellow with the fragrance of flowers. Grabbing an apple from the polished wooden bowl on the hall table, Sara went looking for Elena, the round-faced maid she had engaged, who evidently had already left for the day. After a quick shower, Sara came back to the kitchen feeling marvelously hungry. There was a roast in the warming oven and a tossed salad, along with warm flour tortillas and a pitcher of tangy limeade.

She ate in contemplative silence. The kitchen was a gleaming expanse of shining vinyl floor and modern appliances, with a handsome ceiling fan turning lazily overhead. This beautiful house might belong to any white-collar family, she thought, yet the distant swish of waves breaking upon a silver beach subtly denied this. There was something luxurious about that sound. . . .

She jumped at the sharp rap on the door. As she hastened to answer it, Sara's heart was crowding her throat—good grief, who was she expecting?

Gabe leaned against the doorframe in rangy indolence. "You forgot this," he said, holding out her towel.

Sara simply stared at him. He wore a nubby blue polo shirt and those shabby jeans, and amusement sparked his eyes as she visibly sought her voice.

"I was just leaving, and thought I'd drop it off," he spoke when she could not. "You have butter on your chin."

"Well, thank you, I . . ." Butter on her chin? Should she ask him in? She didn't want to ask him in, she was dying to ask him in! What on earth was wrong with her, she wondered wildly! Such a flux of conflicting desires wobbled her voice. "I appreciate it, Mr. Gabe. Thank you."

The odd look chasing across his face was quickly replaced with his bedeviling grin. "You're welcome. And it's just Gabe." To her consternation, he burst out laughing.

At what? The butter on her chin? Sara hastily wiped it, but he still laughed, seemingly overcome with his private joke. Taking the towel, she gave him her best imperious look, but it was terribly difficult to attain any semblance of dignity while dressed in brief white shorts and a halter top.

"Something amuses you?" she asked frigidly.

"Yes, something . . . amuses me! Oh, Sara, you are delightful!" he exclaimed, his entire face registering that delight.

"And you're impossible. Now goodnight." Aware of his roaming gaze, she studiously waited for him to withdraw himself from her door.

He shifted comfortably against the frame and re-marked, "I don't think I've ever met a woman who does that so well. And such a *lot* of it!"

Further disconcerted, Sara stammered, "W-who does what so well?"

"Blushes. All over, too," he observed.

What little composure she had left was washed away in the crimson tide engulfing her body. His insolent gaze traveled down to her small bare feet and came back up with caressing slowness, lingering on her mouth. So acutely conscious of that powerful male virility that she quivered, Sara stepped back from him, a telling act which was registered in his faintly cynical grin.

Her chin lifted in chaotic defiance. "Thank you for

bringing the towel. Goodnight," she said with enough frost to freeze any man. But this was not *any* man.

He grinned and touched her nose. "Goodnight, Sara. I would very much like to kiss you goodnight, pursue that intriguing disinterest of yours, but . . ." He shook his head, and a lock of dark hair fell over his brow, curling her fingers with the urge to touch it. "I've never been slapped by a woman. I might not like it, and then what would happen? I don't want to take a chance on spoiling our beautiful friendship," he gravely assured.

Sara heard her spontaneous peal of laughter with some astonishment. He looked delighted at her response, and she was jolted at how much she wanted to kiss that curving mouth.

"I'm so glad you're as interested as I in preserving our beautiful friendship, Gabe. Tomorrow morning I fully intend to have you fired. Goodnight." She closed the door without waiting to see if he was out of the way. He laughed all the way down the steps.

Such incredible cheek! Sara walked through the empty house, telling herself that he really had some nerve, as well as several other suitable remarks, but a tinge of joy mocked her already limited sense of outrage. That irrepressible grin absolutely compelled one to laugh with him! She tied her hair in a ponytail and then left the house to take a walk down the beach and watch the sunset, imagining a huge golden stallion and its tall rider silhouetted against the dull orange orb. She would report Gabe tomorrow, she assured herself.

The quality of her solitude evoked deep passages of memories. Sara walked slowly, remembering, smiling at times, feeling a mist of sadness at others. It had been so wonderful once upon a time, she thought wistfully. She had been wrapped in the love and warmth of a family, and the chilling awareness of precisely how alone she now was broke down her defenses. Sara wiped angrily at the tears streaking her cheeks. Good grief, why was she feeling sorry for herself when she had the good fortune to be walking this beach, watching that sunset?

As the first stars came out, she felt tired and sleepy. She heard music from the clubhouse, a woman's laughter soft on the air. For the first time, she felt hurt that no one had come to welcome her to the island. Alex had said that one of the pleasures of this place was respect for a person's privacy, and up until now, she had enjoyed that, but darned if she wouldn't love some of Billie's chatter right now!

She bathed and got into bed, then fell asleep, thinking of dark-lashed eyes as green as summer leaves.

When morning came and Sara examined her intent, delaying awhile seemed reasonable in view of the fact that she was not riding today. She devoted the day to writing letters and various little pleasures, and by evening, the incident with Gabe had assumed its proper perspective. The brash young stranger was merely an amusing paragraph in her letter to Billie, hardly worth the flap she had made about it. Having a man fired from his job simply to satisfy her vanity was not her style, Sara told herself—not over something as meaningless as a kiss! He had probably kissed hundreds of women without complaint. Hadn't he looked astonished at her threat?

That arrogant air of male supremacy was irritating, but likely well-founded. How many women could resist the powerful attraction he so effortlessly exerted? She supposed he could be forgiven for thinking he could have any female he met. And, of course, this was the

Christmas season, a time to be charitable towards one's fellow man. . . .

By the time Sara finished reflecting, she had convinced herself that she'd overreacted and decided to dismiss the incident.

Any sensible person would, and she was a very sensible person.

Chapter Three

The man called Skeet, who apparently had no last name, was middle-aged, rawboned, and given to laconic responses, particularly concerning Gabe.

"Ah yeah, Gabe . . . might say he works here. Comes and goes as he pleases, independent sort of feller," he drawled.

"Comes and goes as he pleases? You permit an employee to do that?" Sarah asked in surprise.

Skeet shrugged. "Well, Gabe's a likable young feller. Real good with horses, too. Ain't all that much to do around here," he said, looking as vague as he sounded.

"Then he does, definitely, work here?"

"Does a right smart amount of work here," Skeet said. He matter-of-factly began saddling the gold mare, and even though she wasn't disposed to riding, Sara was forced to, lest he wonder at her reason for being there.

That afternoon she gave serious thought to inquiring about Gabe at the grocery shop, but Alex called to say he'd be arriving the next day, so she resolutely swallowed the temptation. What would Alex think if he learned she was going around the island asking about a strange young man?

After dinner, Sara put on her briefest bikini and went down to the beach. She saw an older couple in the distance and returned their friendly wave; then they left, and she was again alone in this expanse of incredibly lovely beach. She donned her bathing cap and swam for awhile, but a nagging sense of loneliness slowly dimmed her pleasure. It was amazing how much she hungered for someone to laugh and talk with, to share this pale lavender dusk filtering over a molten sea. Irritably she reminded herself that tomorrow Alex would arrive, and since she would be back to slaving over a typewriter again, she ought to be enjoying this last night of leisure!

Unable to convince herself that she was enjoying anything, Sara floated to shore and came out of the water. She took off the cap and shook out her hair. The hand she raised to smooth it froze in midair as a familiar voice called her name.

The surging gladness romping through her left Sara strangely shaky. He wore white nylon trunks and a red terry cloth jacket, and she was acutely aware of every line of that long, slim body. A medallion on a fine gold chain glinted against the darker gold color of his throat. Feeling almost disoriented by the sensations hammering her heart, she raked a hand through her hair, telling herself she would be cool, detached, her usual composed self, but even as she thought it, her eyes lit with the smile curving her lips in joyous welcome. She was simply too delighted to react in any other way.

"Hello, Mr. Gabe," she called liltingly. "Still just Gabe, or have you acquired another name?"

"Still just Gabe. I'm sorry to see that you've taken to wearing a bathing suit, even such a nice one as that," he sighed. Green eyes roamed lustily over her miniscule suit. He had a way of looking at her which made her feel naked—why had she worn this ridiculous suit!

"I'm dreadfully sorry you're so disappointed. I'm also surprised that you're still here since the last ferry has already left," she pointedly reminded.

"Oh, I'm bunking here for the night."

"Oh? Who with, Skeet? He seemed inordinately fond of you," she said, sounding faintly surprised.

"Umm . . . been talking to Skeet about me, have you?" His gaze twinkled down her legs. "Am I now unemployed, broken to mere stableboy?"

"No, I—well, I decided not to report you." Sara gave a careless shrug, and looked up at him from under her lashes. "I mean, it was just a kiss, hardly something to get excited about. In retrospect, rather amusing, in fact."

"Amusing?" he echoed with steely softness.

Taken aback, Sara shook her head, setting her hair to tumbling about her shoulders. "I mean, the *situation* was amusing. And so were you," she added defiantly. "Surely you didn't expect me to take it any other way?" Her airy laugh came off none to well. "Is it really your nature to just grab and kiss a woman on two seconds' acquaintance?" Her eyes widened—she hadn't meant to say that!

"If I feel like it, yes," he responded evenly.

"And you never get in trouble for it?"

He shrugged, his smile careless. "Not in the way you mean, no. I've found most women amenable to being grabbed and kissed."

"You sound very sure of that, doubtless because of your vast experience with women," she said, sweetly scornful.

"You might say I've had some experience with your sex," he answered in laconic agreement. "I take what's so readily offered. Why shouldn't I?"

Sara's lip curled. *"That* I can believe. However, it's possible that you've mistaken quantity for quality."

Tension suddenly flared between them as his eyes made contact with the fine young breasts thrusting against the brief swim top. "Quantity and quality, in certain situations, are one and the same, I find," he said, sardonically. "Delve a little deeper under those delectable differences and all women are basically the same." The green eyes narrowed to heavy-lidded amusement. "Even to the same instinctive knowledge of how to goad a man into taking what he wants and then reacting with outraged innocence when he follows his instincts."

His voice softened to a silky warning. "And I am a man who follows his instincts, little Sara, never mistake that. That little female trick of intriguing my interest by indifference could be a dangerous one."

Sara's mouth went dry at the implicit threat. Once again, a dangerous man had suddenly replaced the engaging Gabe. Her small, heart-shaped face, up-turned to his, paled a little. "It wasn't a trick. I just don't respond to caveman tactics, that's all," she gamely replied.

"Don't you. A fascinating lack of response, I must admit," he mused. He laughed, and he was the easy-going charmer again. "Come walk with me," he commanded. Taking her hand, he started down the beach.

"You sound like a cynical man," she said hesitantly.

"I prefer to use the word realistic."

Unwilling to be drawn into another frustrating argument, Sara changed the subject. "Where do you live? And what do you, besides clean stables?"

"You have something against menial work, do you?" Gabe mildly asked.

"Oh no, I didn't mean to imply that, I just meant ... well, Skeet said you sort of come and go, so I ... what do you do when you're *going?*"

"Hush. I'm not in the mood for questions," he chided.

"Oh, what are you in the mood for?" As soon as it was out, she regretted it. It sounded provocative. Was it meant to? The hard, warm fingers enfolding hers were having a strange effect on her senses.

Laughing, he let go of her hand and curved an arm around her waist. "I'm in the mood to kiss you again. Several times, in fact. If you want the truth, I'm in the mood for far more than kissing, little Sara."

Surely she ought not to be enjoying this so much. "Stop calling me little Sara—I'm a grown woman," she said crossly. "And has it occurred to you that we're total strangers?"

"Ah, but I've found close encounters with total strangers sometimes the very best kind," he confided, looking wonderfully amused.

"Well, you score well in originality, at any rate," she tartly returned. As she glanced up at that dark, handsome face, it suddenly occurred to Sara that he might have mistaken her status here. While it was possible he was merely attracted to her, it was also possible that such an attractive man knew his commercial value, and was seeking to exploit it. Piqued at the ulterior motive she had just given his attentions, she casually moved from his arm and put a little distance between them, her face sweetly serious as she looked up at him.

"Gabe, I don't know if you're aware of it or not, but I'm not a guest here, not in the usual manner. I'm an employee just like yourself. I'm Alex Brandt's secretary, and he's arriving tomorrow. We're here to work . . ." A rueful smile curved her lips. "To put it bluntly, I haven't got a spare dime," she said bluntly.

The intense green eyes fixed on her. "Now why would you feel it necessary to tell me that, I wonder?"

"Because I thought you might possibly . . . well, it's not unusual for golden young men to attach themselves to wealthy women, is it?" she replied matter-of-factly.

A cynical smile thinned his mouth. "And vice versa, wouldn't you agree? However, I'm well aware of who you are. True, it's a shame you don't have a spare dime, but you do have a few other assets worth considering. And there's the intriguing fact that you swim in a cowboy hat. It's the first time I've encountered that," he drawled.

For a moment, Sara wondered wildly if he had spotted her before or after she was draped in the towel. "It's nice to be memorable, even if only for your swim attire, or lack of it," she said dryly.

"In or out of clothes, you're memorable. Now tell me about Sara and why she hasn't got a spare dime," he commanded with an odd authority.

"For the same reason you don't, of course. I'm just a working girl. And there's nothing to tell. I work for Alex Brandt, I live in New York in a small apartment that I share with another girl. The end. Your turn."

"I can't believe that's all there is to a girl who goes swimming in crocodile-infested pools," he said gravely.

"Gabe, if you could possibly refrain from mentioning that for at least five minutes, I would be grateful," she said testily.

"Would you! How grateful?"

47

Sara stopped and stared at him. "You know, you really are a *lecherous* man," she said in wonderment. "Have you thought about professional help? I hear they're doing marvelous things with Don Juan complexes now."

"Woman, you are impertinent, do you know that? Also edible," he sighed, looking down at the red swim bra. "Now continue with Sara's biography."

Shaking her head in baffled delight, she laughed again. "You get to ask questions, but I don't?"

"Correct. Now continue."

"No. I loathe injustice. If you won't, then I won't."

Gabe swiftly stepped closer, his hands curving around her arms, the compelling attractive face very near to hers. "When I argue with a woman, there are certain ground rules I follow—"

"All right, I concede the argument," she said hastily. She caught a whiff of the cologne he was wearing, and it jerked her heart into a totally new rhythm. Gabe looked so disappointed at his easy victory, that her laughter spilled over as he dropped his hands.

"You have a lovely laugh, Sara. Now, since I won the argument. . . ."

"Okay." Unthinkingly, she took his hand and swung it between them. "I'm an only child, my mother died when I was fourteen, my father passed away a year ago. At eighteen, I graduated from high school, entered secretarial school, waitressed by day, studied by night, graduated—" she gave him a mischievous upward glance. "Cum laude, of course; spent two years at Keenan Publishing, three years with Mr. Brandt. See? Ordinary," she ended ruefully.

"Yes, ordinary." An odd undertone in his voice widened her eyes in question. He stopped and ruffled her hair, his eyes soft on her face.

"And you, Gabe?"

"Ordinary. College—" A teasing grin enchanted her. *"Summa cum laude,* of course."

She made a face at him and took his hand in both of hers to examine it. Tanned and calloused, a strong, competent hand, she thought. Dropping it, she turned from him and asked casually, "You grew up in Texas?"

"Yes, in Texas. In a house with a mother and a father and a big woolly dog. I was mad about the girl next door, and kept snakes in a bottle. See? Ordinary," he mocked. He took her hand and began walking again.

"Gabe? Did you really graduate *summa cum laude?"* she asked shyly.

"Yes."

"Then why are you wasting your life?"

"What makes you think I'm wasting it?"

Knowing she had been presumptuous, Sara ducked her head. "Well, your current job . . . you just seem to me to be a man who could do anything he wanted," she said very softly.

He smiled. "I generally do exactly what I want. And right now I want exactly this, walking hand in hand down a deserted beach with a lovely, albeit inquisitive, woman."

Realizing that she too wanted exactly this, Sara swallowed her questions and kept silent pace beside him. The sea looked so vast and mysterious with the moon just rising up through the waves. It felt very good to have her hand enclosed in his. Perplexed at her feelings towards this puzzling man, she stole a glance at his strong, arrogant profile. He was a stranger, and yet it felt beautifully natural to be walking beside him, feeling his nearness as a velvety caress upon her senses. It really didn't matter who he was or how long she had known him, she marveled . . . not here, not now.

Something her mother had said emerged from the mists of time with startling clarity. *"Someday, my Sara, you'll meet someone, a person of rare quality, and you'll feel it as natural as breathing to take his hand and walk beside him in a harmony that has nothing to do with reality . . ."*

Sara let out her breath in a long sigh. It was madness to connect her mother's words with the deep golden man walking beside her, his fingers curled warm and tight around her small ones. When she looked up at his shadowed face, she saw a smile curving his finely shaped mouth.

A person of rare quality. She shivered and turned her gaze out to sea, fighting the nameless stirring which had nothing to do with reality. The last of sundown looked like molten ribbons of deep orange and gold in a pewter sea and sky. "It's so beautiful," she whispered.

"Yes. Sara, have you ever ridden a horse on the beach at night?"

"No, I haven't. But it looks wonderful in the movies, sort of wild and crazy," she replied with a touch of wistfulness.

His voice was oddly gentle. "You've never done anything wild and crazy?"

She laughed nervously. "Ah no, I'm more of a look-before-you-leap type of person. You know, the one you can always count on to have an umbrella on a rainy day . . ." Embarrassed at the flippancy which did not succeed, she let her voice trail off.

"Want to give it a try?"

"Oh no, thank you, I couldn't . . ." Sara stopped, staring at him. Why couldn't she? She was nearly twenty-five years old and not once had she so much as taken a step without giving thought to the next one.

Besides, she reflected, this all had an oddly unreal quality, as if this island were outside natural laws.

"You mean right now?" she asked uncertainly.

"Right now." Without waiting for her to agree, he turned her toward the slope which banked the houses from the beach area and helped her up into a four-wheel vehicle that was parked under a giant mango tree. These luxurious jeeps were the only cars she had seen on the island, which wasn't surprising; the airstrip and wide sidewalk that linked everything together were the only paved surfaces.

With Gabe laughing at her involuntary gasps, they rocketed over the rough terrain, up hills and over gullys with equal exuberance. When they drew up in front of the stables, Sara frantically smoothed her hair. "Remind me not to get into a jeep with you again, Gabe!"

He laughed again and scooped her up out of the jeep as easily as if she were a child. Then, he led the palomino out and bridled him.

"He's so beautiful. What's his name?" Sara asked.

"*Diablo Oro,* The Golden Devil," Gabe said, looking devilish himself.

"He belongs to the Fieldings, doesn't he?"

"Um hum, he does."

"Do you know him personally, the son, I mean?" Sara asked her question with utmost diffidence. After her stupid outburst the day before, she was distinctly uneasy with the subject, and yet, oddly curious.

"Of course. I work for him, remember?" Gabe said dismissively. He pulled off his jacket and tossed it over a rail. Sara felt a shiver run through her. His skin was a rich, dark gold, perfectly complementing the magnificent horse. She caught her breath as he turned from her. Sleek as satin, his back rippled with muscles, his slim waist tapering into lean hips and thighs.

"You must spend a lot of time on beaches," she said faintly.

"As much as possible," he returned, flashing a grin. "You ever ride bareback?"

"Heavens no!"

"Time you tried that, too. Up you go!" Before Sara fully realized his intent, she found herself sitting on the back of the enormous stallion with nothing to hold on to. Gabe handed her the reins, then swung up behind her, curved an arm around her midriff, and took back the reins.

"Gently, Diablo, we have a lady aboard," he reminded the horse.

Sara found her voice, but it was ignored as they headed out of the corral and into the night. Once she got over her initial alarm, she found it an exhilarating experience. The warm, powerful flesh beneath her signaled every move the stallion made, and she was keenly aware of his great strength and the fluid grace of his movements; of the arm around her waist, holding her in perfect security as the horse broke into an easy canter.

"Like it?" Gabe murmured close to her ear.

Sweetly conscious of the chest cradling her naked back, Sara leaned back into his strength and felt the tight knot of unease release. "It's wonderful! The most exciting thing I've ever done!" she laughed.

"Hang on, here we go," Gabe said huskily.

His arm tightened and drew her snugly back against him. They had reached the beach, and water sprayed around their feet as they raced along the edge. Sara held tightly to Gabe's arm as the horse increased its speed, but she felt no fear. They flew over the silvered sands, laughing, intoxicated with the night and themselves, and the great golden stallion that carried them. Sara had never known anything like this intense delight. Her hair whipped wildly in the wind created by their speed and the air sung in her ears—it was glorious!

When they reached the jumbled black rocks which closed one end of the beach, Gabe reined in the animal, and they sat quietly, watching the moonlit sea. His arms slowly wrapped around her, and she felt his lips, touching her neck with light, butterfly kisses, edging under her hair to the sensitive flesh behind her ear. His breathing on her skin betrayed his mounting excitement. Thrilling to his touch, she stiffened as the warm, caressing mouth moved down her neck in a trail of fire. The darkness pulsed with electric tension, and she felt a strange melting sensation deep inside.

"Sara," he whispered, saying much more than just her name.

The night, the moon, the man holding her, the huge stallion trembling from his run, merged together in erotic enchantment. Sara realized, in an oddly remote fashion, that his mouth grazed her cheek, only because she had turned her face into his.

"I—I think we'd best go now," she said breathlessly.

"No."

His mouth covered hers and reality faded altogether as her lips instinctively parted and clung to his in passionate response. His hands on her skin were warm and caressing, his mouth pressing urgently—

The horse neighed and shook its mane. Distracted by the movement, Sara swiftly broke away from the kiss. Gabe rested his face in her hair while she groped for the scattered threads of reason. *He was a total stranger.* Incredible that she kept forgetting that!

Her shameless response was a deep-felt embarrassment. Seeking to end it as graciously as possible, Sara laughed and said, "We'd best go. I think I've had enough excitement for one night!"

"Are you quite certain of that?"

Disconcerted by the seductive male whisper, she tried another laugh and brushed ineffectually at the arms embracing her. For an unnerving instant, she caught an image of a young woman so securely insulated in a cocoon of her own making, that she had no conception of the devastating power of love and passion. They were only words in a book, one wrapped up in pretty fantasies, the other a superior smile of amusement.

Angrily she thrust aside the unpleasant revelation and replaced it with logic. It was the ride; she had never done anything so wild. Naturally she would be susceptible to such intense excitement. His mouth was warm on her back, then gone, and the absence felt like a chill along her spine. The shy, sweet anxiety filling her was so at odds with her orderly self that she shivered.

"Yes, I'm quite certain. Please, Gabe? I'm really quite tired and while this has been great fun, I—take me home, please? It's the third house—"

"I know which house," Gabe tersely interrupted. Taking up the reins, he turned the horse back towards land.

Sara was obscurely disappointed at how quickly they arrived at her door. Gabe said nothing on the ride, and just as silently got off the horse and lifted her down. She sensed an anger in him that both surprised and alarmed her. Looking up at his dark face, she pushed at her hopelessly tangled hair. He made her feel as awkward as an adolescent, she thought irritably, his tall, powerful figure looming over her with disturbing force.

"Well, goodnight. Thank you for the ride, it was lovely," she said, dismissing him.

The big hands spanning her waist tightened. "Not so fast, little Sara, I'm not finished with you yet," he said evenly.

Her heart slammed against her chest. "W-what do you mean? Let me go—Gabe, stop it!" she cried, struggling against the hands which were slowly, inexorably, drawing her into his arms.

"When I'm ready. Right now I'm going to take the kiss we both want," he said with hardening tone.

His head bent to hers, but Sara turned her face aside, her voice sharp. "No, stop it, Gabe! I don't want any more of this foolishness!"

He gave a low laugh as she twisted in his grip. "Don't you, Sara?" he mocked, and the mouth she sought to avoid caught her denial in a hard kiss. She was trapped against his naked chest, held with muscular arrogance as he ruthlessly plundered the warm, inner sweetness of her mouth. His mastery was infuriating, but the more she struggled, the harder he kissed her, and against her will, Sara felt herself responding to his dominance. The treacherous force of her own desire surged to meet his in a kiss rapidly becoming less punishing and more passionate, sweetened with tenderness as he felt her pliant yielding.

Sensing he no longer needed to restrain her, Gabe gave his hands free play, hungrily exploring the soft body pressed into his. Sara's shocked protest was countered with a kiss taking total possession of her will. Her arms wound around his neck, her fingers curving deep into his hair, holding his mouth to hers in a kind of wild, soaring pleasure that was beyond her experience. Drowning in a blissful flood of sensations, she molded herself against his hard male contours, his sensuous excitement a demand she could not resist. She moaned softly, her hands caressing his warm, muscular shoulders. Groaning her name, Gabe wrapped her tighter and kissed her until she lost all sense of self.

When his mouth left hers, Sara clung to him in mindless protest, until his low, triumphant chuckle stung her ears. Her heart was hammering with hard, painful thuds, her body trembling with the passion he had aroused—and he *laughed!* She wrenched from his arms with a hissing breath of outrage, only to be roughly hauled right back again.

"Let me go!" she gritted.

Unperturbed, Gabe murmured, "When I'm ready." He laughed softly and kissed the corner of her mouth, since that was all he could catch. "Ah, Sara, your indifference enchants me! What a delight you must be when you feel something for a man," he drawled.

"I suppose you think this proves something besides the fact that you'll use brute force to subdue an unwilling woman?" she flung at him with cutting sarcasm.

For an instant, Gabe's fingers dug into her soft upper arms, then, abruptly, he let her go. "It proves that under that frozen virtue hides a very exciting woman," he said with a shrug, sounding bored. "Whether or not it's worth a man's trouble searching her out is another matter. Goodnight, Sara. Sleep well," he ended mockingly. Vaulting onto the horse, he lifted a hand, and horse and rider were swallowed up by the night.

His arrogance left her gasping, but the flick of truth in his words itched like a burr under sensitive skin. As

Sara got ready for bed, she carried on a furious argument with herself. She could not put into precise words just what he had insinuated, but the *feeling* was there, and she fought against it with little splashes of outrage to counter her deeper thoughts. Of course she knew why he had kissed her like that—the masculine need to conquer, thought Sara scornfully. Just because she insisted upon respect from a man and refused to fall into his arms like some giddy little twit didn't make her less of a woman!

And who was he to be passing judgment on *her?* A man who thought all women were alike—she had heard the contempt in his voice when he spoke of women! After all, what was he? Nothing but a, a beach bum! And working as a stablehand was not exactly one of your more dignified careers!

Faintly ashamed at her snobbishness, Sara got into bed and pulled the covers up around her throat in unconscious defense. Tremors of excitement still trembled deep within her as she remembered that demanding male urgency, the sensuous pleasure of his mouth and body, the masterful manner of a man who took what he wanted, knowing it was his for the taking— *because it was?*

She gave herself a hard shake at this discomforting thought. True, she had momentarily taken leave of her senses, but Billie had warned her that sooner or later she would feel the jolt of chemistry that flares between a man and a woman against all reason. Gabe had aroused feelings she hadn't known existed, but chemistry was a clean, sharp word she could handle. Somewhat chagrined at its intensity, she flopped over on her stomach and cuddled down to sleep.

A stray thought penetrated her drowsiness: that she

had to take into consideration her own reckless actions. Twice in two days she had given into behavior so out of character that it could properly be termed aberrant.

"Oh, for heaven's sake, Sara, a ride in the moonlight!" she fumed.

A ride in the moonlight on a golden stallion, held tightly in a stranger's arms, and afterwards. . . .

Sleep did not come easily and when it did, it was all tangled up with dreams she would rather not have had.

Chapter Four

When Alex called the next morning to say that his departure from New York would be delayed, Sara felt obscurely let down. In some way, her employer's arrival would define her life again, give her carefree days the needed sense of direction. Unaccustomed to total leisure, her attitude toward it was ambivalent. On one level, she reveled in the deliciousness of indolence; on another, she was nagged with guilt at such self-gratification.

She saw Gabe's chosen lifestyle in the same ambiguous light. That he was apparently quite happy being exactly what he was, an aimless drifter, altered her conviction not one whit; he had it all—charm, looks, intelligence—and he was cleaning stables! And then only when he felt like it!

Well aware that it was none of her business, and unable to relinquish it, Sara walked to the window and gazed out upon the picture-postcard view. Had Gabe decided to work today or had the allure of sugar-sand beaches destroyed his initiative? She supposed he lived on the mainland; Alex had said that Americans found Mexico a comparatively inexpensive place to live, perfect for retired persons living on pensions and young people scraping along on odd-job subsistence.

Like Gabe. Such lack of ambition in an intelligent young man struck her all over again as nothing less than incredible. How could he endure the natural derision that any well-balanced person—like herself— could not wholly conceal? She knew he had pride, it was implicit in every move he made. Gnawed by such inconsistency, she glanced at her watch, frowning. It was nearly noon and she had accomplished nothing. Decisively, she strode to her room and donned a swimsuit under her jeans and shirt, then struck out briskly for the stables.

Idly, she noted several planes on the airstrip, including the blue and silver one she had seen several times. Having a plane at one's disposal must be the height of luxury, she thought. Sleek pleasure boats bobbed in the marina like children's toys in a blue-water bath. What fun it must be to ride in one, skimming over the waves.

The intrusion of last night's confusing episode was firmly disciplined. It was pointless to dwell on something that did nothing but confuse! It was bad enough that an image of a great, golden horse and its tall rider was emblazoned on her mind. That romantic, almost gallant image of Gabe was an idiot's delight and certainly had nothing to do with the basic man himself.

Only Skeet and the Spanish boy were at the stables. Absurdly annoyed at this, she carelessly inquired, "Gabe isn't working today?"

Skeet glanced at her. "Naw, he hasn't come in yet. Reckon he had business elsewhere."

"But he did stay here last night," she remarked.

"Yeah, stayed on the island last night. Reckon he'll show up when he's ready. You want Alana?" he asked, regarding her with his usual dispassionate demeanor. Sara could not tell if he liked her or not. He probably just tolerated her, she thought ruefully.

"Yes, Alana, please. Skeet, have you known Gabe long?" she asked, following him into the barn. The pretty golden mare gave her an affectionate nuzzle as Skeet opened the stall.

"Long enough. Easy, girl, easy. Gonna ride Miss Tracey today," he soothed the mare.

Suddenly blushing, Sara turned aside, hating her compulsion to question, but unable to resist. "You like Gabe, don't you?" she murmured.

"One of the finest young men I know," Skeet said without inflection. He led the mare outside and boosted Sara up. Wrinkles fanned around his eyes as he grinned and asked, "You like him too, do you?"

"Well, as you said, he's a likable young feller. But then, so is the young man who tends the lawn," Sara laughed.

"Umm. Speak of the devil, here he comes now," Skeet chuckled.

Clad in cut-offs and tattered sneakers, Gabe sauntered around the corner. "Good morning, Sara," he said in that curiously articulate drawl.

"It's noon, Gabe, but good morning," she said shortly. Glancing at his smooth brown shoulders, she turned Alana toward the gate.

Gabe caught the reins. "Have you had lunch?"

"No, I want to go riding first," Sara said. His hair was sun-glossed with dancing highlights. Resenting the unwarranted admiration she felt for a man who laughed at her, she made a move to go on, but Gabe still held the reins, his manner at once authoritative and easy. Obviously last night's scene hadn't robbed him of sleep; there was not the slightest hint of unease in that handsome face. Well, she could be just as casual about it, Sara vowed.

"Tell you what, let's have a picnic," Gabe proposed. He cocked an eyebrow at Skeet. "Skeet, you think you could call the restaurant and see if they can come up with something resembling a picnic on such short notice?"

"You just call the restaurant and request them to rustle up a picnic?" Sara interjected.

Gabe shrugged. "Well, they like me down there."

"Seems everyone likes you," she dryly observed. She glanced at Skeet's unrevealing face, and back at Gabe's insouciant grin. "It's past noon and you've just reported for work. Are you sure you have time for a picnic?" she asked sweetly.

"Do I hear a note of censure in her voice, or am I just imagining it?" Gabe murmured to Skeet with a side-long glance at her pinkening face.

Skeet grunted. "Ain't much doing 'round here today, so you all run along. I'll go see what the restaurant can rustle up."

"Thanks, I appreciate it," Gabe politely assured him. His eyes crinkled. "Now, Sara, it's much too lovely a day to work. Or frown—" he broke off as the boy led out Diablo, bridled but unsaddled. Gabe moved in a startlingly smooth flow of muscular strength and was sitting astride the stallion before Sara had time to blink.

Glancing at her from under incredibly long lashes, the boy said something in Spanish which broke Gabe up. He leaned down and spoke in a confiding murmur. Sensing herself to be the subject of their apparently hilarious discussion, Sara regarded them with such suspicion that Gabe delightedly laughed again. She frowned, more at her own irresolute self than at him. A picnic with Gabe sounded so lovely she shifted uneasily. How could she want so much to be with him! Glancing at the unruly hair curling about his collar, she shrugged in resignation to a solid fact. Cynical and arrogant he might be, but he was still the most attractive man she had ever met. And that masculine assurance challenged her every female instinct—he'd just see how far he got with Sara Tracey, she thought, pleased at the prospect of giving him a setdown.

Tossing her head as her gaze tangled with twinkling green eyes, Sara urged Alana onwards, but the mare looked around in big-eyed surprise, and affectionately nuzzled the stallion's neck.

Skeet appeared just then with a laconic confirmation of the restaurant's willingness to rustle up a picnic. Gabe courteously thanked him, then grinned at Sara. "Let's take a run along the beach while they get it together."

No sooner said than done. The stallion leaped into a trot and Alana followed without regard to Sara's wishes. Her mastery of the mare left a lot to be desired, she reflected, as they trotted after the beautiful horse and rider skimming the sand. When Gabe reined in, Alana obediently halted beside her friend. Gabe reached over and caught Sara's head, and kissed her.

She jerked free. "That's enough, Gabe," she said crisply.

"I disagree, but being a gentleman, I yield the point. Race you to the restaurant?"

"You know it's no race. Alana just follows after Diablo," she accused. She felt ridiculously happy.

"Ah well, it's love, you know," Gabe confided.

"And now you're mocking love?" she sniffed.

His emerald eyes widened to feign innocence. "Sara, you wound me! Would I mock what is indisputably the mystery of the universe? As well as such a delectable source of pleasure!" he added with such gusto, a giggle escaped her tightly compressed lips. He was in irresistibly good spirits, the laughing, teasing, devilishly ornery man who delighted her far too much.

"Oh, let's go see if that picnic's ready. I'm starving," she said crossly.

"After you," Gabe bowed.

"Lovely. Now would you mind telling Alana?" she flashed.

Chuckling, he touched the mare's side with his sneaker. *"Vaya,* Alana," he crooned, and the mare pranced on ahead.

A pretty, dusky skinned young woman emerged as soon as they drew up at the restaurant. Giving Sara an envious look, she handed a brown wicker basket to Gabe with a dulcet, *"Ola,* Sēnor Gabe."

Gabe laughingly replied in Spanish and settled the basket in front of him, then leisurely led the way to the beach.

After a noisy, vigorous swim, they came back to the big black rocks which sheltered their picnic, and dug into the bountiful food with gusto. There were thick roast beef sandwiches and crunchy dill pickles, wedges of cheese and fresh fruit, assorted relishes and a thermos of icy lemonade. Conversation was limited to wordless sounds of pleasure; they were both ravenous.

Once the edge of hunger was dulled, Sara nibbled on a stalk of celery filled with cheese and gazed out to sea. "Gabe, Skeet really likes and respects you," she said reflectively.

"I like him," Gabe replied.

"Well, doesn't that—I mean, don't you feel a sense of obligation? To merit that respect, I mean."

Gabe looked surprised. "I fulfill my obligations to Skeet."

Sara watched his strong white teeth crunch into a juicy apple. "Well, perhaps . . . but what about yourself?"

"Myself?"

"Yes, you have an obligation to yourself, don't you? I assume that someday you'll want a wife, a family . . ."

Gabe eyed her with sardonic amusement. "And you think no decent, self-respecting woman will have me, hum? Like yourself, for instance."

Feeling caught, Sara stiffened. "To be frank, no."

Gabe examined his apple, then tossed it away. "What sterling qualities must a man possess to capture the uncompromising Miss Tracey? Driving ambition? A rigid sense of duty? Vows of eternal fidelity?" He grinned mockingly. "Or would a five figure income suffice?"

"At least a steady job!" she flashed. "And that requires ambition and a sense of responsibility you obviously don't possess. As for that crack about a five figure income, I don't care about the size of a man's income, but what's wrong with setting your sights high?" she added defensively. "Which is, in case you missed it, my original point."

"Oh, I didn't miss it." Gabe leaned back on his elbows and musingly regarded her for a discomforting moment, then shook his head. "Ah, the eternal female compulsion to reform a perfectly happy man. It probably began with Adam."

"I was not trying to reform you—"

"Weren't you?" He laughed and came to his knees. "Sara, you're delightful when you try to combine righteous indignation with guilt," he said gravely. When she sputtered, he fell over backwards, carrying her with him. Jarred at finding herself laying fully on top of him, Sara squirmed against his clasp in a desperate attempt to stop the beginning warmth flowing from his body to hers, but he held her easily enough, the tender smile curving his mouth draining strength from her limbs.

Looking at the round breasts pressed into his bronzed chest, he murmured, "You look like a pearl against my skin. Sara . . ." His voice deepened and held her name like a velvet caress as his hands slowly glided down her back, gently caressing her.

Sara had never before permitted a man to be so free with her body, and a clot of shame disturbed her, but his touch was so pleasing! Feeling as if she were drowning in his glowing green eyes, she made a small sound of protest as he unwrapped the turban from her head and cast it aside. Her hair fell in a silken sheet around his face and shoulders. A hand threaded through it to draw her lips to his, while the other glided down her hips and pressed her against him.

"Sara. So soft, so incredibly soft," he whispered as his mouth sweetly possessed her lips. His arms curved around her, and his kiss was no longer gentle. Urgently his mouth pressed on hers, demanding a response, claiming it . . .

What on earth was she doing! Shocked at how disgustingly easy she succumbed to this man's appeal, Sara jerked free of his kiss. "Stop it, Gabe!"

"Why?" he asked huskily. "Don't you like this?"

"This beach—so public—please, Gabe," she choked.

"No one can see us, Sara. But all right, I have a place we can go," he softly replied.

Sara pulled away and sat up beside him. Feeling confused and shaky, not knowing what to say or do next, she began smoothing her hair. After a quick glance at Gabe, her lashes fanned down to conceal her mingled desires. How had she come to allow him so close to her guarded inner self, and after last night's debacle!

He stood up and reached down a hand to her, his manner supremely assured. A blaze of anger steadied her. "Gabe, I have no intention of going anywhere with you," she said flatly.

The hand slowly withdrew. Gabe sat back down and unblinkingly regarded her. He was in control of himself, she irritably noted, giving no sign of the firey desire still storming her body.

"A changeable creature, aren't you, Sara," he sardonically observed. "A moment ago you were as ready as I—or was I mistaken again?"

"Oh, you know you weren't mistaken," Sara angrily admitted. She took a deep breath and told herself he could be dealt with in a sensible manner. "Gabe, you're very attractive and I can't help responding when you hold me like that. But that doesn't mean anything—" her voice rose at his quirking eyebrow. "Gabe, we've known each other only a few days. I can't make love with you!"

"I thought we'd gotten to know each other pretty well," he mildly responded. "Maybe too well, hum?"

"I don't understand," she said stiffly.

"I think you do. You're the marrying sort, am I correct?"

Sara flushed. "Well yes, but . . . I still don't see your point."

"My point is that the size of my bank balance and my humble position cancels out natural desires. I'm not exactly a prime prospect for marriage, am I," he said with heavy irony.

"That's utterly ridiculous, and a vile thing to say! If I loved a man, it would make absolutely no difference to me what his position was, or how much money he had. I'd be proud to be his wife!"

"A noble sounding sentiment. I wish I could believe it, but unfortunately, my long and varied experience with women—" he shrugged expressively.

"Maybe your experience has been with the wrong sort of women!" she hotly retorted.

"All sorts of women, Sara, from the sophisticated to the fresh-faced little girls like you."

Vaguely hurt, Sara snapped, "I'm surprised you waste your valuable time with girls like me! I'm sure a man of your obvious talents could easily attach himself like a parasite to some woman with more money than brains!"

"Easily. But I happen to be perfectly content as I am." Gabe shrugged, his smile ironic. "It's also possible I possess a grain or two of integrity."

Chastened, Sara lowered her eyes.

"Why are you so disdainful about that sort of arrangement, anyway?" he inquired. "It's simply a reverse-mistress situation."

"And I suppose you know all about *that,* too—I suppose you've got a few tucked away in various places?" she snapped, fired with resentment.

"Perhaps, but that's my business," he said with a level look. "And what's so contemptible about that?

Granted, it's a commercial arrangement, but then, so are most marriages."

"You're comparing marriage with—with that? There's not the slightest commercial taint to love, and love is what makes a marriage!"

"Is it? Most marriages are a bargain between two consenting adults; conjugal privileges for checkbook privileges," he shrugged again, his smile mildly contemptuous. "Which stacks up as a commercial enterprise, love or no love. But I'm not knocking it; it does keep the world going round, hum?"

"That's a despicable attitude about love and marriage, crude, cynical. I feel sorry for you, Gabe. I pity a man who has such distorted ideas about love and marriage!" she choked.

Gabe laughed. "Do you now! Don't waste your sympathy on me, Sara, save it for yourself. Because you too must bargain. You want me as much as I want you, but you can't give yourself to a man just for simple, honest pleasure, can you?" he taunted softly.

"I'm not so sure it would be a pleasure!" she flared.

He flashed a cynical grin. "Don't be so hard on yourself, Sara. I'm sure that with a little tutoring in the art of love, you'd reward a man for his efforts."

She was way out of her depths and she knew it. Casting about for an effective response, Sara looked away from that mocking gaze. Well, she might not have the sophistication, but she did know a feminine trick or two! Her lashes slowly lifted, her eyes wide and vulnerable on his face as her mouth curved in an appealingly soft, gentle smile.

Gabe's expression applauded her efforts, his grin reminding her that he knew every trick in the book. Feeling cornered, she blushed, miserably uncomfortable at her failed ruse. The silence crackled as he waited her out.

"I suppose, given your attitude about women, you intend to remain a carefree bachelor all your life?" she asked coldly.

"Quite the contrary. As you said, I have an obligation to myself, and to others. A man has to have a son to carry on—whatever it is sons carry on—which means a proper marriage, of course. But that's far in the future. I have no intention of putting myself in a cage until I have to."

Gabe rose to his feet. Hands on his hips, his head tipped back in an arrogant stance, he looked down at her, the gleam of green eyes barely visible behind his dark lashes. "Always assuming, of course, that I can find someone who'll have me. Well, shall we get this mess cleaned up?" he asked briskly. "After all, as you nicely pointed out, it's long past noon and I haven't reported for work yet."

Sara was touched by some indefinable note in his voice. Had she hurt him? It seemed unlikely that she could, she thought, glancing up at the tall, powerful man towering over her. Yet, she had come on pretty strong about his lack of ambition.

As artless as a kitten, she looked up at him. "Gabe, I'm sorry if I made you think . . . I like you just the way you are, even if I do disagree with your views on—on many things," she said sincerely, and it *was* sincere, she realized. No matter what she thought of him, she liked him immensely.

He knelt beside her. "Do you, Sara?" he asked with odd intensity.

Her small hand cradled his cheek. "Yes, I do. I think you're basically one of the most likable men I've ever met . . . even if you don't have a last name," she sighed mischievously. "Rather arrogant and conceited, to be sure, a trifle domineering, somewhat—"

She was rewarded for her smoothing efforts by his roar of laughter. "Sara, you have a choice: either shut up or get kissed," he warned.

She got on her knees and set her hands on her hips, laughing up at him. "Gabe, do you know, that's the first time since we've met that you've given me a choice about anything!"

Gabe uncoiled until he was standing over her, his face unreadable as he looked down at the vivid blue eyes and the tumbled hair laying blackly against her luminous white skin. Sara waited, wanting desperately to hear his teasing laugh, to see something besides cynicism in his eyes.

He turned away, his voice careless, dismissive. "Well, enjoy it, Sara, it's not my nature to give people a choice. Finish gathering up the picnic, will you? I'm in a hurry," he said impatiently.

Cut to the quick, Sara blindly crammed items in the basket. "What for? Skeet's surely used to waiting for you to put in an appearance," she said spitefully.

Narrowing green eyes met hers with a hard, varnished smile on his handsome face. "Your nagging is beginning to get a trifle boring, Sara."

"Well, it's for your own benefit!" she snapped.

Looking bored, he glanced at her, then out to sea. "Spoken like a good little wife," he caustically observed. "I'll drop the basket off at the restaurant, then I've some business up the hill. See you, Sara," he said carelessly, striding towards his horse.

Unable to resist it, Sara jeered, "What business? Tutoring, perhaps?"

Effortlessly Gabe mounted his horse, his sardonic grin flicking her like the tips of a quirt. "At the risk of being repetitious, I must again point out that that is my business, not yours. I enjoyed the picnic, Sara. We'll have to do it again sometime." With an ironic smile, he waved a hand and turned the horse inland.

"And good riddance," she muttered. Wherever he was going, she hoped he stayed there!

But Sara soon found her heart and mind furiously at odds. Christmas Eve was intensely lonely in the resoundingly empty house. After a very fitful night, she awoke Christmas morning on the dull edge of depression. With her second cup of coffee in hand, she wandered out to the terrace—and slammed up against the most outrageous bouquet she had ever seen! Crammed into a quart pickle jar was a mad clash of blue hyacinths and firey red gingers, ringed with curly-leaved holly, centered with a sprig of mistletoe, and fragrant with six luminous pink roses.

Sara knelt beside it and tore open the card. *"Merry Christmas, Sara. From your vagabond."*

"Oh Gabe!" she whispered tearfully. When had he brought it? How had he afforded it! The residue of anger and resentment simply melted away. Gloriously delighted, Sara carried the flowers inside and put them in a more suitable vase, then went for a run on the beach.

When Alex arrived at noon the next day, the gamine Sara was replaced by a demure young lady in a proper dress and combed hair. She told him he looked pale and exhausted, and he concurred. After changing into a swim suit, he stretched out beside the pool, giving orders not to disturb him for anything less than an earthquake.

Sara was nonplussed; she had supposed they would plunge right into work. She knew he had already received a handsome advance for his next book, which was as yet an intangible substance. Frowning at her diffident questions, Alex took a sip of his lime and vodka, and waved her away much in the same manner as he would a pesky fly.

Hovering about, waiting for orders which were not forthcoming left her keenly on edge. She was not only on salary, but provided with free room and board as well, and was doing nothing to earn it. Irritably Alex suggested she go for a ride or something, which she did, but her overactive conscience tainted this pleasure, too. Besides, Gabe was nowhere about.

As the week passed without a sign of her insouciant tormentor, she became more and more concerned. When she got up the nerve to query Skeet, he looked vague as usual, and muttered something about the holidays. Sara went back to the house fussing at herself. Obviously Skeet wasn't bothered by the lengthy absence—why was she? Because Skeet didn't miss him, and she did, that's why, Sara glumly admitted. And any thoughts she'd had about mentioning Gabe to Alex were dashed by *this* one's lofty insouciance.

"Oh, by the way, tomorrow night we're invited to a New Year's party at the Fieldings," Alex did remember to inform her. "Have you seen their house? It's that big white one at the top of the hill."

"I've seen it. No one's there, though, not since I've been here. At least I've seen no signs of activity," Sara replied. "Formal or informal?"

"Formal, to the teeth—people flying in from all over. Even a celebrity or two, including me," he grinned. "You brought evening clothes?"

"Yes, I brought several gowns. Who's coming, of the family, I mean?"

"Just the son. It's his affair," Alex said with desultory interest. "Hand me that newspaper, will you?"

Sara handed him the paper that had come on the morning ferry, and then found herself at the stables. Gabe wasn't around. At least this time she didn't pester Skeet with questions, even if she did have to swallow them like a mouthful of marbles!

But the excitement of their first island party provided a counterbalance to her irritation at Gabe's neglect. On New Year's Eve, Sara was dressed and ready to go long before Alex was. Pausing again before the mirror that covered nearly an entire wall of the dining room, she critically inspected herself. Her hair was swept back in a soft chignon, pinned with two pale pink silk roses, and a fragile gold chain sparkled at her throat. The white lace bodice of her dress was sleeveless and low necked, and the chiffon skirt draped with beguiling simplicity down her rounded hips, flowing gently to the toes of her white satin slippers.

The gown, one of Billie's, was chic and expensive, and Sara was immensely grateful for that when they arrived at the Fielding residence. The women who graced the elegant living room were as fashionably turned out as any she'd seen in New York.

It was all rather intimidating. Seeking Alex's reassuring smile, Sara held her head at a haughty angle and walked proudly into the room, and then the breath went out of her in an explosive gasp.

Wearing a white dinner jacket and a red rosebud boutonniere, his dark hair caught and imprisoned the light from an enormous overhead chandelier, and his sea green eyes widened when he saw her. Sara knew instantly who he was. The tall, handsome man striding toward them was now, rightfully garbed in his aura of supreme authority, Robert Fielding, the imperious owner of Isla de Paz.

Gabe!

Chapter Five

"Welcome to Isla de Paz, Mr. Brandt. I'm Robert Fielding," Gabe said, taking Alex's hand in a firm handshake. "It's an honor to meet you—a shame we've always missed each other!" The charming smile turned on Sara, green eyes glinting as he caught the full effect of her sleek-looking gown and utterly furious.

"Sara, you look lovely," he said warmly. His eyes crinkled. "But then you always do," Gabe murmured.

Sara's heart was thrashing around somewhere in her stomach. Groping desperately to collect herself, she tried to form words. Did Gabe intend to mention that they'd met? The entire island probably knew it and was snickering at her denseness! Had they been alone, she would have scratched that charismatic smile to ribbons!

Glancing at Alex, she half sighed. "Mr. Fielding and I have met, only I didn't . . . he never . . . oh, I'll explain later. This is a lovely house, Mr. Fielding," she ended frigidly. Mr. Fielding—Robert Fielding—incredible!

"Gabe," he corrected.

Her mouth twisted. "Oh yes, *Gabe.*" Quivering jello inside, coolly poised exterior, she gave him a dismissing nod and turned to survey the room. Had someone asked her to name one object in it at that moment, she would have been at a dead loss. Her eyes mirrored nothing but Gabe's wry grin.

"You insufferable fraud!" she hissed the first chance she got.

"Now, Sara," he chided with a quick glance around.

Spots of color flamed in her cheeks. "How could you—letting me think you were a stable hand! No wonder you laughed when I—stop it!" she said furiously as he placed a hand on her arm. Feeling purely a fool, wondering how she could have erred so grievously, Sara stalked rigidly through the room to Alex's side.

"Everything all right, Sara?" Alex discreetly inquired.

"Everything's fine. It's a lovely party, isn't it," she gaily replied, and tried to immerse herself in the conversation. But all she could seem to do was steal glances at the tall, slim man who moved smoothly among his guests, every inch the powerful executive, and looking so attractive she despised everything about him.

And this house as well, Sara decided, furiously resenting the sleek, modern decor, and the exquisite collection of crystal and impressive artwork which attested to extreme good taste and the money to indulge it. Beach houses should be small, shabby, mildewed-plastic and cotton-ticking affairs. Beer and gritty hot dogs instead of champagne and caviar, she thought with a stabbing look at the man responsible for shattering tradition.

As stormy sapphire eyes tangled with twinkling green ones, Sara tipped her chin in hot defiance, and heard his low delighted laugh from across the room. She slipped out the elegant French doors and walked down the terrace, so mad she was literally steaming. But it hurt too, she thought confusedly, and accompanying the hurt was a desolate sense of loss.

"Sara?" Gabe came up behind her and touched her shoulder, his fingers burning her naked skin. She twisted violently aside.

"Go away, Robert Fielding! You are the most inconsiderate, arrogant, utterly despicable—"

"Robert *Gabriel* Fielding . . . aren't there any good things on that list?" he asked. "Like charming, intelligent, kind to animals, pleasant-natured, good-looking, even."

"Good-looking I'll admit to, with great reluctance," she said between her teeth. "Did you enjoy your little masquerade, Robert?"

"Um hum, I did," Gabe smiled lazily. "Would you believe it's the first time I've been with a girl who didn't know who I was? Just Gabe, a man—a stable hand! I found it delightful, Miss Tracey!"

"I'm quite certain you did. Something like that would suit your twisted sense of humor! Well, I didn't find it so delightful—I feel like a fool! Pretending you were poor when you're filthy rich, letting me lecture you on ambition and—and responsibility! And when I asked Skeet, he said—*nothing!*" she exploded.

"Now, Sara," Gabe chided. His arms curved around her midriff, and she went rigid. "I'm sorry if you were hurt, but I couldn't deny myself such pleasure. As for Skeet, I kind of made it known that I was very much enjoying my anonymity and he went along with it. Oh come on, Sara, it was great fun and you know it. Would you have been so warm and natural with Robert Fielding?" he asked knowingly.

Remembering that wild outburst about Robert Fielding, Sara writhed with embarrassment. "I certainly would not," she choked. "And take your hands off me. I told you I despise men who think they can grab at anything that crosses their path just because of who or what they are! Or had you forgotten my opinion—my very correct opinion—of Robert Fielding?"

"An odd slant of prejudice, but prejudice all the same," Gabe observed.

"Maybe it is prejudice, but I've met a few like you and I've been grabbed at. Let me go!" Sara cried wildly.

"I grabbed at you as Gabe the hired hand, remember? Ah, Sara, don't be mad, hum? It was a harmless little deception." His voice deepened to a seductive caress. "Sara, sweet Sara, you feel so good in my arms. Meet me tonight on the beach?"

"You're insane, do you realize that? I wouldn't meet you on the—on the moon! From now on, you're Mr. Fielding, whatever, and I'm Sara Tracey, secretary; not up for grabs and not interested in sampling whatever charms you have to offer a woman," she said acidly. "Now let me go!"

"Ah, Sara, how do you know if you're not interested in what I have to offer until you've sampled it?" Gabe teasingly whispered.

The nerve of the man! Sara thought wonderingly. How could anyone be that impervious to another's scorn? His arms tightened to pull her back against him, and a warm, caressing tongue touched her neck, sending treacherous tingles down her spine . . . Sara gulped and caught at her runaway senses. She had been pawed before, she viciously reminded herself. There was no need to create a scene. She bent her head and freed herself from his caresses, all in one smooth movement.

"You really are the most impossible man I've ever met," she drawled. "Don't you understand, Mr. Fielding? I'm really not interested."

"Aren't you? You seemed very interested the night we rode on the beach," Gabe softly countered. Without touching her, he let his lips trail across the back of her neck like sensuous whispers. "You taste so good, Sara. I keep wondering if you'd taste this good all over," he murmured. His cleanshaven cheek touched hers as he wrapped his arms around her. "Meet me later?"

"Find yourself another playmate, Mr. Fielding. As I said, I'm not interested," said Sara. "Now if you'll please release me, I'd like another drink." Pulling free, she walked back inside.

Laughter and music swirled around her ears like a distorted symphony. Avoiding Gabe's gaze, Sara stood sipping champagne and listening without much interest to the conversation. She intently examined the glass she held. "From tattered sneakers to crystal champagne glasses," she thought savagely. What did one have in common with the other?

It was nearly midnight, and confetti and noise-makers were being readied. On the stroke of twelve, the usual insanity broke out. Gabe's kiss was quick and hard, quite acceptable in the bedlam of kissing and hugging.

He moved to the center of the room and held up a commanding hand. "Does everyone have a drink? Then let us make a toast, to old friends, and new . . ." His eyes caught Sara's. "To our honored guests, Alex

Brandt, and Miss Sara Lynne Tracey." He raised his glass in a gesture of warm respect.

Hard, warm fingers suddenly gripped hers as they took up the old, sentimental refrain. "Happy New Year, Sara," Gabe said very softly.

"Happy New Year, Gabe. Oh, by the way, thank you for the Christmas flowers," she replied, and abruptly turned from him.

Once the wild elation had settled down to lighthearted merriment, Sara moved away to examine the large, ornately framed painting of a magnificent palomino standing with head lifted and ears alert, against a backdrop of misty blue mountains. The attached metal plate was inscribed, *Regalo de Oro*.

"Gift of Gold. Do you like him?" Gabe asked just behind her.

As she slowly turned to face him, Sara felt explosive with the churning press of emotions, but there were many eyes watching them, and she couldn't reveal even a flicker of distress. Pasting on a brittle smile, she regarded the picture, and answered with the stiff, impersonal manner of a butler.

"He's magnificent, of course. As beautiful as your horse."

"In a way, he is my horse. Gift of Gold was the sire of all our palominos. The Fieldings settled in California when it still belonged to Mexico, and Gift of Gold was just that, a gift to my great-grandfather, along with two mares in foal. The mare Alana is from the same strain."

"California? I thought the Fieldings were Texans?" Sara asked, interested in spite of herself.

"Some are. There were two Fielding brothers. One decided California was becoming too tame, so he went to Texas to try his luck."

"And his luck was very good," she added derisively.

Gabe's mouth tightened, but he graciously overlooked her rudeness. "You might say that. At any rate, he claimed the foals and carried on the breeding once he'd found a place to settle. For some obscure reason, he chose West Texas, which is not a gentle land. Every time he drilled a well for water, he kept getting this black oily stuff," he said, trying a smile which Sara ignored. "Later he moved further south and built a home, began raising cattle along with the palominos . . . I trust I'm not boring you?" he asked dryly as she half turned to look about the room.

"Why no, of course not," she generously assured him. "Do go on."

A muscle ticked in his jaw, his voice flattening a little. "I have the ranch now. It's west of Houston. I still raise palominos, some cattle—"

"But what exactly do you do, besides play with your horses and cows, I mean?" she interjected.

His face closed, flinting green eyes accepting her spitefulness, and the contest of words used like subtle weapons. "Well, there's the Fielding Corporation, of course, that occupies much of my time." He shrugged, studying the painting. "But I have outside interests, too. My playing with cows and horses has a purpose. You could say the palominos are for pleasure, I suppose, but personally I think such a magnificent strain as *Regalo de Oro* is worth preserving. As for the cows, cattle breeding is a genetic art, and an important one. Well, never mind. Suffice it to say I think what we're doing is a trifle more than playing. Would you like another drink?" he asked with cold courtesy.

Sara's offensive wavered. Always well-mannered and sensitive to others, she felt discomfited by her rudeness. "No, thank you. Please tell me more about your interests. I didn't mean to belittle them, and I apologize," she said quietly.

Privately she derived more pleasure in watching his animated face and gestures than from the subject. Sara had never personally met a cow and didn't much think she'd want to, but the beautiful horses kindled imagination, and it was exceedingly difficult not to be drawn into Gabe's enthusiasm.

Seeing Alex approach, Gabe lowered his voice and asked, "Sara, will you meet me on the beach later tonight?"

Sara was visibly jarred at his audacity. "Sorry, Gabe. Hello, Mr. Brandt, and yes, I'm ready to leave!" she said in saucy resignation. Glancing at Gabe, she gave a merry laugh. "When Mr. Brandt gets that wild, woolly look, it means only one thing: his brain has come alive and is sending out entire chapters!"

Alex grinned his sweetly abashed grin. "Sara knows me far too well," he told Gabe fondly.

Sara extended her hand. "Well, goodnight . . ." she paused, suddenly unsure what to call Gabe. *Mr. Fielding* sounded asinine after their experiences together, yet *Gabe* sounded arrogant somehow. The carefree Gabe who loved beaches and moonlight rides and worn blue jeans had little in common with this tall, distinguished executive.

As if sensing her dilemma, Gabe took her hand and lightly squeezed it. "Gabe," he said firmly.

Sara nodded and echoed, "Gabe. Goodnight." Doing her best to ignore Alex's sidewise glance, she withdrew her hand and picked up her evening bag. "Ready, boss," she said lightly.

Had she carried it off? She thought so. Gabe had a hardness in his eyes, and she had the feeling he would have liked to slam the door behind her! As they walked home, Alex said, "You want to tell me about having already met Gabe, hum?"

"No I don't, but I suppose I'll have to." Briefly she supplied the basic facts, omitting as much as possible, but relating it with such drollness that Alex found it hilarious.

Ambling along beside her, he said gruffly, after he'd stopped laughing, "Sara, you know I'm genuinely fond of you. I wouldn't much like seeing you hurt. Gabe Fielding is a very smooth, sophisticated, somewhat cynical man, as befits his years and experience. And I've got to admit, he's a real charmer . . ."

"Agreed, but what has that to do with me?" she asked coolly.

"Oh hell," he muttered. "Look, my sister Lila says he was engaged to a woman named Moneta Lorenz, that two days before the wedding day they broke up, and the parting was not amicable. According to Lila, it affected Gabe deeply. Maybe he still loves her; certainly he's still bitter about it. Again, remember this is Lila talking, not me. I don't engage in gossip," he stated.

"So why are you doing it now?" Sara asked tonelessly.

"*Because,* that's why!" Alex barked. "I did bring you to this island, and naturally I feel responsible for you. Gabe's got a devilish reputation with women—the looks, the money, the name . . ." he shrugged. "It's only natural. But Moneta's back, and according to the same questionable source, ready to take up where they left off. So far Gabe's playing it cool, but who knows? She's a looker, Lila says, a rich little blueblood who's got it all."

Sara hated to think she was so transparent that Alex felt required to intervene in her affairs. But apparently she was. "Maybe I'm not hard and cynical, Alex, but I'm not exactly a starry-eyed little innocent, either. I have no illusions about Robert Fielding," she assured him. "But thank you for caring, Alex," she ended on a softer note.

They finished the walk in moody silence. Once in bed, Sara lay in hot, itchy self-annoyance, her thoughts buzzing around in maddening circles which resolved nothing. She was not ordinarily given to indecisiveness. She had been in control of herself far too long to abide this turgid confusion, yet the bewildering kaleidoscope of thoughts refused to come to order. Remembering all too well the deep, languid arousal of his kisses, she flung on a robe and stole into the moonlit garden.

The air smelled of lemon blossoms, and the sea was a faint, tremulous stirring in her blood as she pondered tonight's stunning revelations. Down below the darkened houses, the beach gleamed silver in the pale white light, and she wondered about Gabe the insouciant drifter, or Gabe the wealthy Texan—which would she have met on that beach tonight?

Despite her brave assurance to Alex, Sara found herself drifting into soft, dangerous thoughts of Gabe Fielding—as she was doing right now, she realized, snapping to with a start. Alex had placed her in sole charge of the party he was giving tonight and she didn't have time for star-gazing. Gabe was coming to the party. She had seen him only once since New Year's Eve in a chance meeting at the club. He had been clad in a formal gray suit and a brusque, businesslike manner, giving her a chilling glimpse of the formidable man who walked in Gabe's shadow.

Not a man likely to be jilted by any woman, Sara thought longingly. Annoyed at this constant furtive wonder of a private affair, she went to find Alex. He was sitting at the pool side talking to Janet Farr, a winsome brunette in her early forties. Sara waved at them, but did not intrude. Janet was divorced, and in his cherubic way, Alex was an attractive and likewise unattached man. The two seemed to have hit it off and were spending a lot of time together.

After a luxurious bath, Sara put on a satin slip, then a semi-transparent fantasy of watercolor blue and lavender flowers on a misty green background that drifted around her enticing curves. The dress was too outrageously feminine to accept a casual, loose hairstyle, so she pinned her hair high at the back of her head in a severe coil, then pulled loose several long tendrils to dance about her cheeks in a delicious defiance of such primness.

Deriding the excitement shining in her eyes, Sara was forced to admit that she felt something special for Gabe Fielding, a very disturbing something that blithely ignored his reputation with women. An alarmed sense of self-preservation asserted itself; this was merely a late-blooming case of school girl infatuation—Lord knows she was about due for one, Sara thought gaily. However, it would be prudent to avoid his weakening influence as much as possible tonight. She must not risk making a fool of herself, and as giddy as she felt right now . . .

Sara soon discovered that avoiding Gabe's influence was similar to standing in a rainstorm and dodging raindrops. She was conscious of his every move, and unerringly singled out his deep, vibrant voice no matter how loud the hubbub in Alex's living room. Gabe was a dangerous mixture of men tonight: the soft-spoken, imposing Texan and the charmingly roguish Gabe, an irresistible combination to which everyone around him was helplessly responsive, including Sara.

"By the way," he murmured in a private moment. "You still mad at me for that little deception, hum?"

"No, I've forgiven you. Everyone enjoys a good laugh now and then," she said airily. "Besides, having a last name adds stature to a man!"

"Especially such an impressive one, hum?" he murmured.

"Oh, well, of course! Would Gabe Smith be as appealing?" she laughed. Having already turned from him, Sara did not see the curious pain flickering in Gabe's eyes.

"Does it really make all that much difference?" he asked mildly.

"How could it not?" Sara retorted.

Just then a radiant whirlwind of a woman swept into the room, trailed by several attractive young men and women. She paused, and looked around with an eager, expectant air, her countenance lighting as she spotted the one she sought.

"Moneta!" someone cried in the hush.

Sara froze, her hand caught between Gabe's big ones. She glanced up at his face, which looked startled, then flowed into a smooth, pleasant mask as the woman headed his way.

Moneta had cornsilk hair arranged in careful disarray around a face so exquisite that it took one's breath away. She wore a simple white gown with a matching mink stole dangling over one shoulder, and Sara could only stare at her and think how truly beautiful she was. This silver-misted vision was Gabe's fiancée? She made every woman in the room look drab as a fishwife.

Flinging her arms around Gabe's neck, Moneta

exclaimed, "Hello, Robert!" with a shower of impetuous little kisses about his face. Her shiny red mouth bowed into a luscious pout as he groaned and laughingly removed her arms. Moneta promptly wound them around his waist and gave him another kiss, this time on his clefted chin.

"Moneta," he groaned, "what on earth are you doing here? I thought you were supposed to be in Mexico City this weekend," he said indulgently.

"Darling, I had this mad impulse to crash Mr. Brandt's party—I *adore* him!" Moneta prettily claimed, favoring Alex with a dazzling smile. Naturally he reacted just like any man, Sara thought, watching him dissolve. Moneta shrugged off the stole and someone thoughtfully caught it before it reached the floor. Flawless honey-gold skin gleamed with the luster of satin in the lamplight, softer than the fur she so carelessly discarded.

As Gabe belatedly introduced the two women, Moneta smiled with angelic sweetness, and extended a silver-nailed hand. "Mr. Brandt's secretary, right? How lovely! You look just like a secretary and Mr. Brandt looks just like a fascinating, world-renowned writer! Oh I do love it when people look exactly like what they are!"

Somehow Sara was gently eased aside as Moneta took Gabe's arm in casual possession and drew him along in her wake, looking up at him with seductive invitation in those dark, laughing eyes. Soon they were surrounded by the handsome young people who had swirled in with Moneta like the tail of a comet, apparently all mutual friends. Gabe's smile was warm, his voice gentle as he responded to her apparently witty comment.

Covertly watching them, Sara was agonized with

wonder concerning the relationship between these two attractive people. *Did* Gabe still love her? If so, knowing that tall pride, he must be tormented by this elusive little woman. Yet, Sara let herself cautiously admit, he didn't *look* tormented. In fact, he looked like he was having a wonderful time. As for Moneta, perhaps she didn't love Gabe enough to be his wife, but she certainly wasn't about to set him free; that air of possessiveness was a classical example of dog-in-the-manger, Sara thought savagely.

Someone placed a hand on her arm and for a startled instant, Sara was too rattled to recall the warmly smiling brunette's name. "It's Janet, dear," she chuckled. "Listen, Alex and I have planned a marvelous weekend—have you heard of the Houston Livestock Show and Rodeo? Alex has never been, have you?" Sara shook her head. "Well, it's nothing less than fantastic and we're all going the weekend after next," Janet gaily informed her.

"I'll have to think about it," Sara said, looking to Alex for instructions. He grinned adorably and absently nodded. Seeing the abstracted expression that signified two levels of independent thought, she gave a helpless shrug. "I'll really have to think about it," she repeated.

"All right, dear, but do think about it seriously," Janet urged.

Agreeing to consider it strongly, Sara pasted a brittle smile on her face and rigidly concentrated on her duties as hostess. This raw feeling of jealousy was a new and devastating experience, and it required all her wits to combat it. Moneta was the center of attention, her quick-silver quality drawing like a magnet anyone who came within range. She was small and perfectly formed, peculiarly like an enchanting child in many ways, and her melodious laugh tormented the ears with its pleasing sound. Even Sara felt the pull of that dazzling charisma.

Hanging on his arm, her sparkling face continuously seeking his, upturned to within seductive kissing range as Gabe lowered his head to listen to her sweet, breathless voice, Moneta imparted her ownership in a way no woman could mistake. Helplessly watching, Sara was engulfed in a wild, desolate cry of pain that had no voice nor made itself known to those around her, yet the strength of it jerked her heart with physical force. She had been deluding herself—it was not some silly infatuation she felt for Gabe Fielding. *She loved him! A very real love, deep and undeniable once it surfaced, the kind of love that just is.*

She felt an awesome surge of this overwhelming emotion as she looked across the room at the man who owned her heart. And always would, Sara thought, and this in itself was terrifying, to know that regardless of how cheaply he valued that heart, she could not reclaim it. Buffeted by a truth that left her nakedly exposed, she went to the kitchen to refill ice buckets.

Gabe cornered her there a few minutes later and murmured, "Sara, after this is over, will you meet me at the mango tree? I feel in need of some fresh air, a walk . . ."

She froze, torn in too many directions to immediately respond. *He wanted her tonight, not Moneta!* Sara felt a sweet, hot slash of triumph so savage that it shook her. It smoldered in her eyes as she coolly replied, "Yes, I'll meet you."

"Bring a bathing suit, okay? We might want to take a swim," Gabe suggested with another devastating smile.

Wishing she didn't feel so foolishly happy, Sara agreed, and smoothly moved from him. She took great care that he received no undue attention, but an exchange of glances was enough to shake her heart with gladness. Nothing could dampen her euphoric state of mind, not even Gabe and Moneta dancing cheek to cheek on the shadowed terrace. Moneta meant nothing to him, it had been Sara he chose tonight, she reminded herself.

For what purpose? a practical inner voice hounded. "To swim and talk and just be together," she retorted, and the desperation in that was enough to create doubt for a moment. Was Gabe capable of using her to get back at Moneta? Angrily she shoved it aside. She was young and in love and common sense hadn't a chance against such formidable opponents!

What seemed to be an eternity later, Sara stood under the huge mango tree, clad in a brief bikini and an excitement that hammered her heart. She moved into the shelter of its branches and anxiously waited, struggling to block out the creeping tendrils of sanity. Would he come? Maybe he had forgotten—

The night was bright with moonlight, yet the big gold stallion appeared so quickly, she gasped aloud. Gabe reached down a hand to her and swung her up to him, an awkward maneuver, but soon things were as they should be. His strong arm around her, they rode easily this time. When they reached the tiny cove that was accessible only by splashing through the water and edging up between the huge rocks which rimmed it, he dismounted and lifted her down.

Gabe removed the blanket from Diablo and spread it over the still warm sands. "Madam," he bowed.

Warily Sara looked at him. "I thought we were swimming?"

"All in good time. Right now, you sit down, I have a surprise for you."

"Oh good, I adore surprises!" Sara sat down on the prickly blanket and watched while he opened the satchel strapped around his waist, and extracted a bottle and two plastic glasses. "What is it?" she asked.

"Just wait and see, impatient one," Gabe chuckled. Kneeling, he poured a little of the liqueur, then instructed her to take a small sip, then hold it under her tongue.

Knowing she didn't much like liquor of any sort, Sara warily obeyed. It was tasteless, odorless . . . and then, an explosion under her tongue! Firey, delicious, whispering of wild strawberries and apricots and aromatic roses, the brandy went down like a breath of summer air.

"What is this?" she gasped.

"Something very old, very rare, something special for a special occasion. Happy anniversary, Miss Tracey," Gabe murmured.

Sara felt giddy with joy. "You remembered," she sighed.

"Um, it did occur to me that we'd met one month ago today, yes." Gabe stretched his legs and contentedly sighed. "Good?"

"Oh yes! May I have some more?"

He laughed deeply. "Easy, little bird, this stuff's dynamite."

"I can't believe anything that tastes so lovely could get you drunk." Guardedly Sara leaned back against his knee. "Gabe, were you surprised to see Miss Lorenz tonight?"

"Not really. Moneta is the most impulsive creature on the face of the earth. I've learned not to be surprised by anything she does."

"Have you known her long?" Sara probed harder.

"Quite a while, yes. Her parents and mine are very good friends," Gabe idly responded.

Sara gazed at him searchingly. Surely he was aware that she knew of the broken engagement? "I've never met anyone like her. She's enchantingly beautiful."

"Yes," he said rather impatiently. "Sara, you're the only woman on my mind tonight. If I'd wanted another, I would be with her. Let's dispense with Moneta."

"All right, Gabe," she said, concealing her reluctance to do so.

They sipped brandy and talked in low, relaxed intimacy. A big white moon rode high in the sky, and the sea whispered around them, sensuous, romantic, combining with Sara's basic innocence to create an enchantment so fragile, one wrong word would have shattered it.

Gabe said nothing to destroy the mood. His moves, as his voice, were soft and gentle; a hand caressing through her hair, a feathery touch on her face, a fingertip tracing the knobs of her spine one by one. She turned her face to his with a chiming laugh, and he kissed her.

Caught up in the sorcery he created, Sara sat perfectly still while he kissed her, sweetly, gently, nibbling around her lips with deliciously soft, tantalizing kisses. The glass fell from her fingers and she tangled them in his hair as a surge of primitive delight flamed through her. He pulled her into him until she touched all along his lean, taut body, and the thrilling sensation of warm, naked skin coming together was stunning.

The blanket scratched her bare back as he pressed her down into it. Dropping her hands to his shoulders, Sara tensed, waiting for the careless move that would shatter the haze of rapture and shock her back to her senses. But Gabe was too experienced not to sense her apprehension. A master at seduction, he did nothing but kiss her for a time, the same soft, tender kisses, nebulous brushes of fire on her face, her neck, the shadowy hollows beyond, letting her control the situation until she ached to be kissed with passion. An expert maneuver by an expert at lovemaking, and she knew this in some remote fashion, but it didn't matter.

His mouth covered hers and began a slow, sensual kiss that drew her down into a floodtide of erotic delight. Sara blindly tuned to the heady excitement of his aroused body, pressed close, her softness melting into every long, unyielding line of him. Gabe groaned and caught her crushingly tight. Hungrily, he kissed her, his mouth forcing open her lips, demanding her response with heartshaking urgency. She could only cling and give him her ardent response.

His hands were on her breasts, boldly knowing, moving down in a caressing sweep that took her breath. "You taste so sweet, Sara . . . like flowers and women and honeyed wine . . . so sweet," he said huskily.

"Oh Gabe . . ." Whatever else she might have said was forgotten in the heated rush of desire emanating from beneath his caressing hand. Her head arched back, offering her tender throat to his nibbling, tormenting mouth while she murmured wordlessly, delightedly. Everything was blurred by the sweet, firey excitement drugging her senses. Expertly he played on them, arousing and stirring her until she moaned against his mouth.

"Sara, now—I want you now," he groaned thickly. Only the timbre of his voice penetrated her reeling mind. Sara pulled his mouth to hers with a shocking need for his kisses as his body pressed her down into the yielding sand, his excitement a torch lighting the flames engulfing her in a wildfire of passion. The blanket, the sand, was rough and giving—his body was warm. Hands began tugging at her tiny bikini.

A woman's laughter, and then her voice, came from nearby. Sara heard it only as a discordant sound in the music of the night. Her eyes flew open as she heard it again; two women, she realized. "Gabe! Someone's coming—"

"No, Sara, no," he said thickly. "They're way up the beach; sound carries here. Besides, they can't see us, you have to wade into the water to reach this place. Sara, ah, *Sara* . . ." Feverishly he reclaimed her lips.

Sara knew he was right; they were perfectly safe from exposure. But one of the women was Moneta. She recognized that sweet, clear voice riding the wind. Shame scalded her, as well as savage jealousy—how many times had he known this same firey passion with Moneta!

"Sara, don't," Gabe muttered angrily as she twisted under him.

"No, please, Gabe, I can't—they're out there whether or not they can see us! Please?" Sara pleaded huskily.

Swearing softly, fiercely, Gabe rolled aside and stood up. Sara got to her feet and nervously smoothed her hair, looking up at him imploringly. When she shivered in the brisk sea wind, he put his jacket around her, then shook out the blanket and strode to the horse.

"Sara, I find you extremely desirable and a pleasure to be with, but I don't like coy games. The next time you agree to something like this, you'd better be prepared to carry it through," he said flatly, his voice a lash of the anger evident in the rigid set of his body.

"I didn't agree to—I thought we were just . . ." Nothing else would come out. Sara was too confused

95

and embarrassed to think straight. She supposed he had cause to be angry. She *had* been playing a game, but not the one he'd insinuated, she thought dully. Her game was self-delusion, willfully forgetting his carelessness with women, and creating something lovely from common physical attraction. What would have happened had they not been interrupted? A far worse shame than this!

Feeling utterly wretched, Sara quietly accepted his boost onto Diablo. Gabe bounded up behind her and steered the animal toward the water again. Once in the clear, he gave Diablo his head, and by the time they passed Moneta and her friend, they were racing the wind.

Gabe walked her to the door, the cold, stiff reserve emanating from him a harsh indictment. "Here, this is yours—I got it for you," he said, jamming the bottle of brandy into her hands. She knew the flash of teeth was a twisted grin. Looking into his dark face, Sara took a deep breath. He could be so intimidating at times!

"Gabe? I'm sorry that I . . . well, that I disappointed you," she said uncertainly, not at all sure that was what she meant to say, but knowing that his silence demanded something.

He shrugged. "Yes, I can say the same. Good night, Sara."

Diablo and his rider gleamed like tarnished silver in the pale white light as Gabe turned back toward the beach. Where was he going—to Moneta? No, he wouldn't do that, Sara thought, desperate to believe it. But he had left aroused and angry, and he was not a man accustomed to denying himself.

Sara went wearily to bed. She had much to think about, but every line of thought came to a dead end. She knew that a future with Gabe Fielding was impossible, that the woman he selected as a wife would be one of those beautiful, sophisticated creatures of impeccable lineage and position, like Moneta, or someone similar. She knew, too, that any woman who fell in love with him was asking for heartache if she loved too deeply, because he was a man who did exactly as he pleased—hadn't he himself said so? She knew all of this with the logical, reasoning part of herself, and yet her heart spoke only three words: *I love him.*

Sara turned out the light, wanting the darkness because in the darkness everything was softer. She tried to be flippant, thinking to herself—so it has come at last, this perplexing thing called love, it has come even to Sara Tracey, who wasn't at all sure that it existed; thinking—well, it must not be fatal, others have survived it, look at Billie, a new case every few months; thinking—*I love him.*

Chapter Six

Realizing she was supposed to be working, but had in fact, been staring blindly at the same paragraph for the past five minutes, Sara gave herself a mental scolding and sent her fingers flying over the keys. It was annoyingly difficult to keep her mind on the task. Was this what love did to a person? She felt shy and uncertain, gripped with anxiety at knowing her happiness was subject to the whims of another, and if this was love, she didn't much care for it. As much as she resented Gabe's talent for shrugging off bothersome matters, she envied it. The rapturous time she had spent in his arms was indelibly etched on her mind, blazing up when least expected, a torment in the still quiet hours of night.

"Enough, Sara," she ordered, and resolutely set her mind on typing. At least she was an expert at this.

Unbelieving, Sara looked at the last three lines she

had typed. Gibberish! One key off for three whole lines. "Oh boy," she muttered. Ripping out the sheet, she inserted a clean one and began all over again. It had been ten days since Gabe set foot on the island. Why? The press of business? Or perhaps pleasure too enticing to forsake for even the hour or so it took to fly here? She tore out the ruined paper and patiently inserted another.

"Why don't you give it up, honey," Alex fondly advised.

"Oh! Oh, Alex, I'm sorry, I'm all thumbs, and I mean that literally! I know you want this typed by this evening," Sara said distractedly.

"No hurry. I've decided to revise those last two chapters, and I can work from the rough draft. Run along—scoot! Go swim or ride or something," he ordered.

It really was impossible not to hug him! Clasping her hands in her lap, Sara cast a rueful look at the paper littering the floor. "Thank you, Alex, I think I will. Obviously I'm accomplishing nothing here," she sighed.

Alex laughed and waved a hand in dismissal. He certainly was in good spirits lately, Sara thought. Janet's influence, no doubt. Changing to jeans and a polo shirt, she arrived at the stables to find Alana already saddled and waiting. "Mr. Brandt called ahead," Skeet explained. Dear Alex!

She left the path behind and headed Alana deep into the cool, shadowed woods, past the pool which would ever be special, away from the stream and up into the outcropping which flanked the remnants of an ancient volcano, dead since the dawn of history. As she came out on a level plateau, Sara stopped and gazed around her. It was an eerie place, a wild, barbaric, awesomely lovely place, filled with wind-sculpted stones as black as obsidian, squatting like sentinels amid little hills and humps of land dotted with slender green cypresses, the whole ringed with thatches of yellow ginger and what looked to be white satin poppies. And in the distance, the sea; long, undulating combers rolling in like crumbling antique lace on iridescent silk. This must be one of Gabe's wild places, she thought delightedly, imagining a small, green-eyed boy playing his isolated games among the stones.

Deriding herself for getting fanciful, she reined in Alana and opened the thermos for a cold drink of limeade. The mare found her own refreshment in the juicy green grass ringing a tiny seep of water. They rested in companionable silence for a time, then Sara urged the horse onward. The golden light of late afternoon was blindingly reflected from every leaf and rock with little bouncing flashes which dazzled the eye. Wishing she'd worn sunglasses, Sara turned the mare downhill, toward the shade beneath the trees.

Once on fairly level terrain, Alana settled into an easy gait. They were following a wide trail which was bordered by dense shrubbery on one side, and low stone ledges overlooking the gradual panoramic drop to the next level. A lacework of vines formed an overhead canopy and everywhere, those hoary, lichen-covered stones dominated the scene. Totally absorbed in the picturesque view, Sara gave Alana her head as they descended into familiar territory. The breeze made delicate windchimes of the brittle eucalyptus leaves, a lulling sound, soft, whispering.

Just as they rounded a sharp bend, the mare gave a shrill cry and reared so abruptly that Sara was nearly unseated. The next few minutes were mad confusion. She had a dazed impression of something springing up beside them, a long, brown blur she could not identify. Desperately she fought to control the bucking, plunging horse, but she lost the reins and could only grab frantically at the saddlehorn as Alana bolted in wild-eyed fright.

The thermos flew from the pack and hit the ground with a clang. Reacting to the sound with insane alarm, Alana turned sharply and raced at terrifying speed down the crumbling slope, and it was all Sara could do to stay on her. A limb whipped the Stetson from her head and her hair spilled down, half blinding her. Crouching low against the horse's sweaty gold neck, she shielded her face against the low-lying branches and hung on for what seemed an eternity.

Only when they came out on the plateau in sight of the barns did Alana slow down enough to recapture the reins. Sara sawed brutally at the mare's tender mouth, and managed to bring her to a halt. Both sobbing, rider and animal rested for only a moment; Alana was too wrought up to respond to directions. Despite Sara's efforts, the mare obstinately struck out for the stables at a fast clip. At least she was under control, Sara thought hysterically. She had never had such a frightening experience!

Gabe was standing with Skeet and two other men just in front of the barn. As they came around the corner into the corral, Alana stopped so fast, Sara nearly went over her head. Clinging dazedly to the saddlehorn, she saw Gabe with surging joy. She opened her mouth to call his name, but the man coming toward her was stone-faced with outrage.

"Oh, Gabe!" Sara got out before she was lifted

roughly to the ground. He immediately turned back to the trembling mare. Sweat-glossed and sides heaving, her eyes rolling whitely with her shuddering breaths, Alana shied from even his familiar touch. "Easy, girl, easy," he soothed. When his blazing eyes lit on Sara, she shrank back in bewildered surprise.

"You stupid little *fool!* What on earth possessed you to ride her like that!" Wheeling to the stableboy, he began issuing orders in a hard, slashing voice which was obeyed with alacrity.

Too stunned to function, Sara sat down on one of the big, round stones which defined the yard. Gabe thought she had deliberately run the mare to this shocking state? Disbelieving, she stared at him, but his attention was focused solely on Alana, and Sara was still too breathless to adequately explain. She concentrated on calming her own racing pulses while she struggled to understand his furious reaction. The other two men shifted uncomfortably as her confused gaze turned to them. Sara got to her feet and walked up beside Gabe.

"Gabe, I didn't—something spooked Alana and I couldn't stop her. I lost the reins and it was all I could do to hang on! I saw something just as she bolted, something big and brown—I only got a blurred impression of it."

"There are no *big brown things* on the island, Sara, just as there are no crocodiles," he retorted. "Hand me that blanket," he added to the boy.

"Might be Sam's dog," Skeet offered, referring to one of the guards who regularly patrolled the island. "His old Doberman got loose this morning, hasn't come back yet."

"Surely she'd have sense enough to recognize a dog," Gabe snapped.

Even the men looked abashed at his contemptuous tone. Skeet shifted as he glanced at Sara's face. "Maybe, like she says, she was a mite too busy for recognizing anything. Sam's old dog is well-trained, wouldn't bark or chase after a horse—knows better'n that. Probably just asleep when she come on it," he doggedly went on.

As much as Sara appreciated his defense, it only made her feel more embarrassed, particularly since Gabe simply shrugged it off. Humiliated to the brink of tears, she took a step toward him, then stopped, feeling she had run full tilt into an icy green wall as his eyes briefly touched her face. Sara drew an extended breath and pushed at the wild tangle of her hair.

This situation had gotten entirely out of hand, she thought, and she was determined to do something about it! Angrily she caught Gabe's arm. "Now you listen to me—" she began.

Gabe jerked away. "Get out of the way, Sara," he said impatiently. "I'll listen to you later, right now I've got to see to the mare."

She felt like she had just been slapped!

Gabe abruptly turned his back to her and knelt to run his hands over the mare's legs. Her cheeks burning, Sara glanced at the embarrassed men, and let her hand fall to her side.

"Yes, of course. I'm sorry, I hope she isn't hurt, I—" It was then that she saw Moneta standing in the shadowed barn door. Whether or not she had been standing there all this time or had just stepped out, Sara didn't know, but it was a mortifying shock. Clad in a smart black riding habit, with a honey-hued Stetson perched on her gilded head, she stepped outside, leaned against the side of the barn, and idly struck her boot with her riding crop. She offered no greeting, just smiled silently.

Sara was drenched by a hideous wave of embarrassment far sharper than anything she'd felt thus far. Literally afire with it, she fought down the surge of nausea and looked helplessly at Gabe. His back was still turned. In the hot afternoon sunlight, the four people who filled Sara's vision seemed to blur and sway gently, then coalesced into sharply etched outlines like photographic negatives.

Sara shook her head sharply to clear it. She glanced at Skeet and thought she detected pity in his eyes. Her chin went up. "Excuse me," she said in a voice flat with pride. She did not look at Moneta again.

Head held high, Sara walked through the yard without a backward look. Hot tears stung her eyes and then spilled over as she struggled to maintain her proud carriage. It would not do to let Alex see her like this, and by the time she reached the house, she had regained a measure of composure. Hoping she looked as calm as she sounded, she gave him a brief summary of the incident, then went to the bathroom and unceremoniously threw up. Everything was just catching up with her: her fright, Gabe's raw anger, the agony of being humiliated in front of Moneta. Weeping silently, she filled the tub with uncomfortably hot water and lowered herself into it.

Everything ached, including her heart. And her pride—how it smarted! Enough to dry her tears and gift her with the saving grace of indignation. To think she had actually fancied herself in love with such an inconsiderate and unfair man! His horse was all he cared about, he hadn't given Sara's distress a second thought!

He hadn't even asked if she was hurt. It was a desolating thought.

She toweled off and dressed in a white cotton gown trimmed with lace and pink satin ribbons, and tied her hair at her nape. It gave her a fragile look, which was just how she felt, she bleakly reflected: bruised and fragile enough to break if handled roughly. As she recalled Moneta's amusement, a soft moan escaped her. Resolutely she pushed it from her mind. It had happened, and dwelling upon her sickening abasement did nothing but flay her already mangled pride.

She would not think of Moneta, she vowed, but she couldn't help wondering if she had come with Gabe, or with one of the other people who flitted to and from the island like a flock of restless butterflies. Evidently she and Gabe were going riding when she made her dramatic entrance—had they gone after she left? Oh, what did she care what they did, either of them!

Alex was on the terrace when she came out. "How are you feeling?" he asked, looking at her searchingly.

She realized he had some vague notion that she had been insulted and he ought to avenge it and he was dreading the prospect.

"I might have to sit on a cushion for a few days, but I think I'll survive!" she laughed and replied teasingly. Deliberately she turned the conversation to the beautiful area she had discovered today, describing the fascinating rock formations, the lovely sense of peace and quiet she had felt—before Alana took it into her head to go home in such a hurry, she ended with a giggle. Alex's relief was so visible, she giggled again, and gave him a droll description of herself clinging to Alana's neck like a flea on a dog.

Her smile froze as Gabe walked around the corner.

Alex got up and diplomatically blocked his way. "Hello, Alex. I'd like to speak with Sara," Gabe said tersely.

"I'll have to see if Sara feels up to seeing you. She had quite a fright this afternoon. She's not an accomplished rider, and trying to handle a runaway horse is not exactly a pleasant experience," Alex said in mild rebuke.

"Oh, of course I'll see him. Hello, Robert, what is it, please?" Sara called. *Gabe* was a special name to her, not to be given to the hard-faced man she'd met this afternoon, she thought with icy resentment. She would not call him Gabe again until he had redeemed himself —at least a little!

Gabe waited until Alex closed the door behind him before replying. Evasively his eyes touched on the innocent white gown, the satiny hair curling around her face. It was the first time she had seen Gabe at a loss for words. In another, less assured man, she might even think him uncertain.

Giving no quarter, she prodded. "Robert?"

"It's Gabe," he said with a weak parody of his familiar grin. "Sara, I came to apologize. I lost my temper and I didn't give you a chance to explain. I'm sorry."

"Accepted," she said without warmth. "How is Alana?"

"I think perhaps she's pulled a ligament in the left foreleg. I've a vet coming in the morning. I'll stay over until then, and then I've got to go back."

"Is Moneta going back with you?" Sara couldn't resist asking.

"Yes, she and her mother rode down with me, so naturally they'll be going back with me," he replied impatiently. He shifted, an odd hesitancy in his manner. "I . . . meant to ask, you weren't hurt, were you?"

"No, I wasn't hurt," Sara said without inflection. "Not physically, anyway." Her eyes chilled. "And something did spook Alana—maybe the dog, I don't know. As I said, I was far too busy just trying to hang on to her to pay any attention to anything else, but I wouldn't deliberately ride a horse to that condition—"

"Sara, I know that. I'm quite certain that something spooked her and that you were powerless to control her—she's always been a highstrung animal," Gabe interrupted. "Look, I was upset, in a temper. If I doubted your word about the dog for a minute or two, well, I didn't know there was a dog running loose, that's strictly against orders. I was wrong, and I apologize. Now can we forget it?" A glint of humor sparkled in his eyes. "After all, I had reason for doubt; you do have a very active imagination," he teasingly reminded her.

"I suppose all 'stupid little fools' do. Well, as you suggested, we'll forget it. Goodnight," Sara said coldly, and turned in cutting dismissal.

"I just said I was sorry about that!" Gabe snapped.

She didn't reply.

"Very well. Goodnight," he said evenly.

As he walked away, Sara stared at that arrogant back with a volatile mix of anger and hurt. "I even lost my cowboy hat," she said bitterly.

Gabe slowly turned around. "Sara, cowboy hats can be replaced," he said as if speaking to a petulant child.

"Not this one! But trust you to think so—what does one stupid hat matter when there are countless others exactly the same, performing the same service. Why should one be special!" she flung at the hard green eyes.

Gabe knew that what she was saying had nothing to do with a hat. A host of expressions crossed his face, then his mouth drew thin in a confirming smile. "I couldn't have put it better," he drawled.

"Oh, get out of here!" she spat.

He stiffened, smiled again. "That was my intention." Touching his fingertips to his brow in a mocking salute, Gabe left.

Sara walked to the back of the terrace, hands clenched as she swallowed her sobs in frantic gulps. She felt she had been dealt a physical wound. What a fool she was, she thought contemptuously, mooning over him, believing against all evidence to the contrary that he saw her as a person and not just another female body to warm his bed! Gabe Fielding was no different from the men she had met in New York, her mangled pride soothed. She had simply let the soft, voluptuous aura of this island influence her thinking and *make* him seem different. As for loving him, there was nothing she could do but conceal it as best she could, and hope that no one saw through her pretenses. A sensible course in every way.

A long sigh accepted her verdict. It was that moment of dusk when the wind dies utterly and everything has the soft, translucent quality of a Chinese brush painting and grips the heart with poignant pain; like the heaven and hell of loving a man, she thought, and oddly enough, her mood was perfectly suited to the evening.

Three very long days later, so at odds with herself she snapped at Alex for no reason, Sara took her unstable self from the house before she did some real damage. She knew that Gabe was on the island because she had seen his plane arrive late yesterday evening, but he had not come to the house. She both dreaded and anticipated the inevitable encounter; the pain he had so uncaringly inflicted upon her was a hard, frozen lump in her chest, and Sara felt she no longer knew herself well enough to predict her reaction.

As she strolled around to the side veranda, the blue and silver plane glistened in the sunlight. Feeling dangerously explosive, Sara decided to vent some of her frustration with a vigorous walk, perhaps even a ride. Facing Skeet would be uncomfortable, but she had to do it sooner or later, she grimly admonished, and it might as well be now.

Skeet's hawkish face was devoid of expression as she entered the stables and greeted him in the usual manner. On the surface, nothing was amiss, but she waited uneasily while he saddled not the palomino mare, but a large roan stallion which she devoutly hoped she could control.

"He's spirited, but gentle," Skeet said, suspecting her fears.

"He's beautiful, Skeet. Oh, by the way, did the guard's dog ever come back?" she carelessly inquired.

"Yep, came back that night. Gabe gave Sam the devil about it—he don't like dogs running loose what with the horses and such. Just them little poodles on the island, usually," Skeet said disdainfully. Glancing at her set face, he went on in musing tone. "You know, Gabe's right fond of that little mare. He had a younger sister, must of been fifteen years younger'n him. Gabe thought she hung the moon . . . died when she was just sixteen, water skiing accident. Anyway, Gabe went'n give her a newborn colt for her fourteenth birthday . . . she named it Alana. Makes that mare kinda special, don't you see."

"Yes, I see," Sara said, almost inaudibly.

"I was kinda surprised when he let you ride her. Not many folks git that privilege. You ready to go?"

"Yes, I'm ready. I can mount by myself," she said when he offered a hand.

"Yep, been noticing you're gittin' to be a regular eques-trienne," he grinned.

Sara suddenly felt she had a friend in this steadfast man, and her soft, shy smile reddened his face. "Thank you, Skeet," she said warmly.

Skeet shifted. "You're welcome. Enjoy your ride," he replied in his best laconic manner.

Sara rode back to the vicinity of her mishap and spent several fruitless hours searching for her hat. It was late afternoon when she returned to the house. Alex was out and she was thankful for a reprieve from pretending. Running a bath, she scented it with a light rose fragrance, and sank down into the silken water with a tired sigh.

It was all very well telling herself that she didn't give a fig what Gabe thought of her, but her heart knew better. If she could only align it with her mind, she'd be much better off! Superimposed over the image of the delightfully roguish Gabe she had first met that sunny afternoon was the image of a forbiddingly angry man who kept his priorities straight. When it came to a horse he loved and a girl he'd kissed several meaningless times, the horse won hands down.

She was not going to permit what Skeet had divulged to influence her in any way, although she couldn't help feeling a little better at knowing the reason for Gabe's unthinking anger. Being cursed with a soft, tender heart, she could easily absolve him every wrong and play the fool again. Closing her mind to everything but the selection of something to wear, she got out of the tub and listlessly prowled through her closet, at length taking down a slim white skirt and a peony pink shirt, simply because they were at hand. The skirt was loose around her tiny waist; she had to start eating properly. Even Alex had commented on her lack of appetite lately.

Coiling her hair atop her head, she went to the small formal living room that doubled as her office, and set to work with unflawed attention. When Alex peeked in and suggested dinner at the club, she declined. He had dictated several letters, and it felt good to attend to duty.

Her fingers froze on the keys as she heard Gabe's husky voice requesting entry from Elena. Aggravated by her fast heartbeat, Sara swiveled around in her chair and watched him striding across the room.

"Sara," he said pleasantly.

"Good evening, Gabe. Alex isn't home, but I think you can find him at the club."

He carried a pair of riding gloves which he slapped across his palm as he looked down at her. "As you well know, I didn't come to see Alex. I thought perhaps we might take a ride—"

"Sorry, I'm too busy. But thank you for the invitation," she replied with impeccable courtesy.

He shot her a sharp, angry look, and strode to the window. "Sara, you are one problem I can blasted well do without!"

"Believe me, I am not one of your problems," she coldly replied. She was suddenly fed up with love and him and this whole darn mess!

"Aren't you?" he laughed harshly. "Aren't you now . . ." Silence crashed between them as he gazed out upon the lovely view of the sea and sky and big black rocks.

"No, I'm not, and neither are you one of mine. In fact, I'd prefer not to see you again," Sara stated without rancor.

Green eyes narrowed as he looked over his shoulder. "Sara, may I remind you that you are a guest on this island—*my* island—and are thus expected to behave accordingly? The decision of whether you see me or not remains my prerogative."

Sara was startled. "Your prerogative? You mean you'd actually force me—"

Gabe's dangerously soft voice sliced through hers. "I never use force on a woman. I find simple, common persuasion quite effective." His tone flattened. "But I will not be insulted by a timid little mouse who suddenly decides she's capable of belling the cat!"

Sara regarded him with a spark of humor. "What on earth are you talking about—mice and cats and bells?!"

"What I'm talking about is . . . what I'm talking about is the simple fact—" Gabe rubbed the back of his neck. "Who knows," he ended disgustedly. "Look, I've admitted I was wrong, and I've apologized. What more do you want of me? I'm not accustomed to begging."

"Nor to admitting you're wrong, I'll warrant! That arrogant pride of yours could hardly admit to being wrong about anything! Well, for your information, you're obviously not accustomed to apologizing, either, because I've had better apologies from a New York cab driver!"

Gabe swung around, amusement lighting his face. "Okay, point taken. I most humbly apologize for everything. Now come for a ride with me."

Sara stared at him, marveling at this quick change, as well as his confidence that since he had humbly apologized, her ruffled feathers were therefore smoothed, and they would now go riding! "No thank you. Alex didn't bring me to the island for my pleasure, nor for yours," she said stiffly. Swiveling around to her desk, she began typing again, with dismal results. "Oh, *foot!*" she muttered, and ripped out the hopelessly botched sheet.

His low chuckle went all over her. "Sara, stop sulking now and come on. Alex isn't going to get uptight if you take an hour off."

"Whether or not Alex gets uptight isn't the issue. I do have a sense of responsibility, Robert, at least when it comes to work," she said smartly. "Excuse me, please?" Dismissing him, she inserted another sheet of paper and typed with maniacal fervor until his hands came down on hers.

"Now stop that," he arrogantly chided. "You're behaving like a silly child."

"Robert—" Sara said in a dangerously high voice.

"And if you call me Robert again, I'm going to kiss you," Gabe pleasantly warned.

"And if you kiss me again, you're going to get that slap in the face which may well spoil our *beautiful friendship!*" she furiously mocked.

With a delighted laugh, he leaned down and kissed her.

Her slap sounded like a shotgun going off in the quiet room.

"Damm!" Gabe exploded.

"Well, I warned you!" Very near tears, Sara glared at him, her mouth a tremulous pout.

He rubbed his cheek and experimentally worked his jaw. "So you did. You pack quite a wallop for such a little thing. But I'm happy to announce our friendship is still intact. You coming quietly, Sara Lynne?"

He was simply incredible! "No I am not! I told you I

had work to do. Now if you don't mind, I'd like to get on with it, Rob . . . Gabe," she ended much more meekly as his eyebrow slanted in warning.

Gabe shrugged. "All right, another time then," he said lightly, and walked off with that beautiful arrogance she so loathed and loved.

Of course, she hastily reminded herself, there was the fact that he had permitted her to ride Alana. That counted for something, though she wasn't sure just what. And as he so snidely pointed out, she was a guest on the island. . . . Not even to herself would she admit her blind yearning to go with him.

Just as he reached the door, she said imperiously, "Just a minute, Gabe, I'm going with you. Well, it's a woman's prerogative to change her mind, isn't it? And I feel like a swim." Daring him to make a crack, she stood up and smoothed her skirt. "Well?" she challenged.

"I'm delighted that you've changed your mind," he said suavely. "Meet you in ten minutes at the stables?"

"Ten minutes will be fine," she haughtily returned.

Gabe's mouth twitched. "I can give you fifteen if need be."

"I said ten minutes would be fine!"

Inclining his head, he said, "Yes, ma'am," but she caught the grin on his mouth as he turned from her.

"Arrogant wretch," she muttered as the door closed behind him. A burst of laughter on the other side stung her ears.

Fumbling with haste, she put on a demure one-piece suit, rather like a clinging chemise over brief panties. The filmy red and pink fabric had the brilliance of stained glass, and looked smashing with her dark hair and ivory complexion. And if Gabe so much as laid a finger on it, he would get another slap; that last one had been marvelously satisfying. Timid little mouse, was she? Brushing out her long black hair into a wanton romp of curls swaying around her shoulders, Sara struck a provocative pose. Since they were playing a game at which she had no experience, it was time she imposed a few rules of her own!

Remembering how easily he could shatter her composure, she was momentarily overwhelmed by the depths of her innocence. Why hadn't she paid closer heed to Billie's advice, and discarded her unapproachable manner and gained some solid experience before tackling a man like Robert Fielding! Adult games called for a form of deceptive skill she did not possess, she thought forlornly. But Gabe didn't know she was such a novice! Her chin lifted. She was sick and tired of everyone, including Alex and even Janet, thinking her a child so dumb they had to hide the matches lest she get burned, Sara thought with grand and quite confused defiance. She would learn to play with fire if it killed her! Beginning this day, she would show Gabe Fielding that she was as worldly as any woman on the island— and far from a timid mouse!

Gabe was just entering the barn when she arrived. She greeted him quietly and stood aside while he opened Diablo's stall. "Shall we ride double?" he inquired.

"No, I'd prefer not to. The brown mare will do," she politely assured. Alana snickered softly and nudged her shoulder. Turning, Sara fondled the soft gold nose, speaking nonsensical words with genuine affection.

"She's still a bit lame," Gabe said matter-of-factly.

Sara lowered her eyes to hide her longing. If only he would confide in me the reason Alana is so precious, I could say I understand, and maybe everything would be all right between us, she thought. She stepped away from the mare. "Yes, I know. It wouldn't matter if she was or not, I don't intend to ride her again." Thanking Skeet for his assistance, she mounted the mare and rode out of the corral ahead of Gabe, but he soon caught up with her, then set the pace.

He always would, Sara thought wanly. Until he lost interest.

Chapter Seven

Winded and water-logged, Sara splashed through the shallows and flung herself on the soft, ferny bank. Gabe came down beside her, his eyes gleaming deeper than the pool, his shout of laughter a song on the afternoon air. As he reached for her, she reeled to her feet and began towel-drying her hair. A blade of grass between his strong white teeth, he leaned back on his elbows and watched her steadily. As far as he was concerned, everything was back to normal, Sara thought irritably—at least, *his* version of normal.

"It's a shame you didn't have your cowboy hat—you wouldn't have gotten your hair wet," he observed, carefully observing her reaction.

"Yes, a shame. I hated losing that hat. It was very dear to me," she said softly. "Billie gave it to me as a going-away gift when I left New York."

He shrugged. "Well, maybe it'll turn up . . . who's Billie?"

"One of the loveliest people I know," she replied, and told him about the roommate she so adored—of Billie's generosity during her father's extensive illness, and of her sympathy and support when he'd died.

"She sounds like a very lovely person," he gently agreed.

"She is," Sara said shortly, refusing to be moved by his tender smile, or the joy of sharing Billie with him. That scene at the stables with a spitefully amused Moneta looking on was still a bitter shadow at the back of her mind. Maybe he had dismissed it, Sara thought, but she never would.

She walked to the saddlebag to get her hairbrush, and perched on the ground-hugging limb of a nearby tree, and began brushing her hair in contemplative silence. The water play with Gabe had been a pleasure too joyous to resist, but it was only a temporary lapse, she anxiously assured herself. He was in such wonderful spirits. The merry, teasing Gabe she loved so much was a bittersweet torment to her heart which ached to respond to him.

Gabe flipped onto his stomach. "You look like a wood nymph sitting there." When she made no reply, he idly inquired, "Are you looking forward to the rodeo this weekend?"

She shrugged. "Oh, that. No, I decided not to go with Alex and Janet. Three's an awkward number, despite their protests to the contrary."

"But I'm making it a foursome," Gabe said. "It's all been arranged. You and Alex are to be my guests for the weekend. I'm meeting you there either Friday night or Saturday morning, depending upon my own schedule."

Nettled at such highhandedness, she made a face. "I see. Why didn't someone consult me before it was 'all

118

arranged'? I'm not certain I want to be your guest. After all, such a magnificent gesture must have a price tag, and it's possible I'd prefer not to pay it.''

A surprised look flitted across Gabe's face. Searchingly he studied her, and what he saw tugged at his mouth. The wind had caught her hair and feathered it around her heart-shaped face, giving her a soft innocence which belied the cynical smile accompanying her words. Unaware of this effect, she held her pose until he looked away.

His drawling response set her teeth on edge. "Aren't you jumping to conclusions? Taking you all the way to Houston for seduction purposes seems an inordinate amount of trouble. Unnecessary, too. If I put my mind to it, I imagine I could accomplish it right here."

"My, you do display an exorbitant amount of confidence in your prowess," Sara chuckled. Wishing it didn't sound so artificial, she tipped her head and regarded him through sun-dazzled lashes. "Women are capricious creatures. It never pays to be too sure of yourself, Mr. Fielding," she said in a low, sultry challenge.

He laughed, a touch of devilry glinting in his eyes as he lazily murmured, "Shall we put it to the test, Sara?"

Suddenly aware that her eyes were on the lean figure stretched prone on the grass, Sara made an effort to shake off its effect. His trim white swim trunks enhanced his superb physique, she thought angrily, catching his knowing grin. She detested that look in a man's eyes!

She stook up and tossed the hairbrush onto a towel. "It's just possible the test might disillusion you, Gabe. You're an attractive man, I admit, but hardly irresistible. And I'm not overly susceptible, despite your opinion to the contrary," she said crisply. Flinging back

119

her hair, she gave him a brilliant smile. "New York has its own charming egoists, you know," she loftily continued. "Many just as handsome and appealing as you assume yourself to be."

He laughed softly. "And you've had your share, hum, Sara?"

Sara colored at the insolent barb. "Let's just say I've met a few of your caliber, Mr. Fielding, and came out on top—I mean I—oh, shut *up!*" she hissed as his laughter rocked the air.

"Top or bottom, which ever way you ended up, I don't think you've bested too many men, little Sara," he taunted.

Stung to recklessness, she snapped, "At least I've never been jilted!"

An eyebrow arched. "Jilted?"

"Yes, jilted, thrown over, cast aside, whatever you want to call it! I heard about your engagement to Miss Lorenz!"

"Ah. What else did you hear, Sara?"

Something in his voice suggested caution. Not too comfortable with this, Sara drew herself up and said, "Repeating gossip is not a habit I indulge in. I think we'd best go."

"I think we'd best not. What else, Sara?"

The soft, steely voice riveted her in place. "Just that you were deeply affected and were still . . . bitter about her leaving you," she said with visible reluctance. Gabe's eyes were dark and narrowed, and she quailed at what he might say next. Why had she started this! Knowing herself outclassed, she made an appealing little gesture meant to convey her self-disgust, and took another step toward the horses.

To her astonishment, he burst out laughing. "Oh,

Sara, the things I learn from you! Here I thought that Moneta and I had simply decided we weren't quite ready for marriage yet and that we were on friendly terms, but instead I find that she jilted me and that I'm now a bitter, defeated, absolutely shattered man!"

Crushed by this roundabout way of confirming his friendship with the beautiful Moneta, Sara would have given anything for a clever retort, but the best she could manage was a weak, "It's possible I was in error. I was acting on secondhand information. I must admit you're not quite the portrait of a bitter, absolutely shattered man." Her voice chilled as his amusement deepened. "I'm sorry I said anything. It's not my nature to pry and I seldom concern myself with gossip, particularly when it doesn't interest me. I don't know why . . . I'd best get back home," she decided.

Gabe gathered up the towels and followed her to the horses. "Sara, the trip to Houston has no ulterior motives. I admire Alex Brandt and it would be an honor to have both him and you as my guests for the weekend. To be frank, I was looking forward to showing you two Houston," he said with a disarmingly boyish grin.

He gathered up a handful of her damp, silky hair and drew it across his mouth, his voice husky. "I fully intend to make love to you, luscious little Sara, but I prefer accomplishing it on the merits of my indisputable charm." The cocky, mischievous grin twisted her heart. "I'm simply an immensely nice, generous man who enjoys making magnificent gestures without any strings attached—and I'm one certainly not accustomed to paying for a lady's favor," he continued. "There now, changed your mind about me? Taking back all the mean things you were thinking, hum?" he crooned.

Clenching her hands against that dangerous charm, Sara forced a laugh. "Taking it under consideration," she said tartly. "As for the lovemaking, that's still very much in doubt. Your charms may be indisputable, but they're not overwhelming. And I don't feel all that flattered about being invited to join your harem, either."

Sara transferred her attention to guiding the horse through the fringing willows and out onto the trail. Had she injected just the right amount of scorn into her voice? Deciding she had done splendidly for a novice, she took the lead with a gay laugh.

Coming abreast of her, Gabe glanced at her from the corner of his eye and chuckled. "My harem? You're equating me with Diablo, hum?"

"I couldn't have put it better," she said sweetly. Her rueful little sigh was perfection. "More gossip, I'm afraid, but taken into context with the man, it has a ring of truth in it." Wondering how long she could keep this up, she coughed to soften the knot in her throat.

"I thought you didn't concern yourself with gossip?" Gabe taunted.

"I find this entire subject boring and refuse to discuss it any further." Sara rode ahead a little ways. "Besides, you're overestimating yourself if you think you're as handsome as Diablo!" she tossed over her shoulder.

His laughter rode the soft, singing wind. Glancing at the laughing green eyes and wind-mussed hair, Sara thought she had never loved him so much.

A few minutes later, they reached the stables and she discovered how swiftly love can reverse itself. As soon as they dismounted, Gabe began chatting with Skeet while she stood waiting, awkward and uncertain, a part of the woodwork for all his attention. When she turned and walked out of the barn, Gabe broke off his conversation long enough to call, "Bye, Sara. I'll see you in Houston," before turning back to Skeet.

Stony-faced with resolve, she walked swiftly down the hill. Janet and Alex were lounging at the pool when she entered the house. Wearing her brightest smile, by now as easy to don as her shoes, Sara walked out to join them. The conversation was relaxed and enjoyable. The warm rapport between them lightened Sara's heart, and soon her laughter was genuine.

"Oh, by the way, why didn't someone bother telling me I had changed my mind about going to Houston this weekend?" she asked, making a joke of it.

Janet waved an airy hand. "Oh, darling, we were going to, but Alex said something about a mile-wide stubborn streak, so Gabe commanded us to let him handle it. I assume he did?"

"In his usual highhanded way, yes," Sara said, annoyed that they had discussed this behind her back.

"Yes, he is a wee bit highhanded," Janet complacently admitted. "You mustn't hold it against him, Sara. It's as natural as breathing to Gabe. Comes from all those years of having his every whim catered to . . . fawning, some might call it. It goes to a man's head after awhile. Take dear, sweet Alex here . . ."

Sara laughed and gave up her annoyance. Leaving Alex at the mercy of Janet's deliciously barbed wit, she went to run a bath, pondering the complexities of the Houston weekend as she soaked in the fragrant water. Gabe's trips to the island were always unexpected, and she rarely spent more than a few hours in his presence. How was she going to handle an entire weekend with him in constant attendance?

His negligent farewell still chafed, and Sara's soft mouth set. She had never done anything so extravagant as fly off to another city simply for pleasure. It sounded like fabulous fun, and she was not going to let his presence spoil this new and exciting experience. "So help me, I won't," she assured the dubious blue eyes in the mirror.

The lobby of the Regency Hotel soared thirty stories high, and Sara was abashed when Alex caught her craning her neck much like any tourist in New York. Slim and chic in her winter white pantsuit, she stood regally beside him while they registered, but another unique feature of the hotel, an elevator with glass walls, soon ruptured her pretense. As the lobby dropped away, the sensation of rising nakedly through thin air visibly whitened her face, and left her stomach lagging further behind with each floor attained.

Alex's teasing chuckle flooded her face with color. Janet curved an arm around her shoulders, scolding, "Shame on you, Alex." He looked properly ashamed, but Sara was too busy swallowing to enjoy it.

The handsome young concierge who guarded the twenty-ninth floor greeted them with an affable smile and the softly slurred drawl she had come to associate with Texans. After unlocking the door to her suite and courteously ushering her inside, he led Alex and Janet on down the hall. Sara closed the door, and stopped with an audible gasp as she looked around the opulent white and gold room. A handsome spiral staircase led up to the bedroom, which opened out on the thirtieth floor. Her luggage was stacked neatly on a rack in the plush dressing room, and a bouquet of mixed flowers spilled their fragrance. "Good grief!" she muttered vexedly, this was surely beyond the limits of good taste. She didn't want to think about what this was costing Gabe!

When she walked down the hall to Alex's room with as yet unassembled protests in mind, his matter-of-fact acceptance of Gabe's hospitality made anything she might say seem distressingly gauche.

"These are Texans, Sara," he explained, as if that said everything.

Sara felt like contesting it, but just then Janet opened the door of a similar suite and strolled in with a suggestion to which he readily acceded. A few minutes later they were in the glass elevator again, mercifully deposited in the lobby without Sara's having embarrassed herself, and were then escorted to a long, black car which whisked them off to a vast shopping mall called the Galleria, where Janet owned a shop.

Leading the way through a series of boutiques within a boutique, past furs and evening gowns, casual wear and heavenly lingerie, they reached western wear, and what Janet referred to as a rather poor selection of elaborate satin shirts and designer jeans.

"It's all so picked over," she fretted.

Picked over or not, Sara was soon resplendent in a celestial blue shirt with pearl buttons and tasteful rhinestone accents on shoulders and cuffs, and a pair of jeans that fit like supple snakeskin. Everyone agreed they were absolutely made for her, and they left for the bootery where a pair of honey beige calfskin boots with alligator uppers were likewise crafted just for her slender feet.

Anxiously Sara sought Alex's eyes—who was paying for this? She had seen the price of the boots, and she didn't have that kind of money! Serenely perturbed by her demanding look, Alex picked up the packages and followed Janet through the mall to a men's shop where they replayed the scene, with him as star this time.

"Darling, don't worry about it, it's all taken care of," Janet airily commanded when Sara ventured a question on the subject.

Taken care of? By whom? It seemed the height of crassness to pursue the subject. Sara toured the handsome mall with them, and even managed to enjoy a soft drink at one of the little tables flanking the ice skating rink. Janet, looking elegant in a simple cashmere sweater and matching wool skirt, was in fine form, and Alex's enjoyment was contagious. Sara smiled to herself as she followed them to the car; Alex was several inches shorter than Janet, but neither seemed to have noticed it.

"We're meeting Gabe at seven for dinner—informal, but I always think *The Quantum* requires a nice dress," Janet said at their respective rooms.

Everyone seemed to forget that she was from New York, one of the fashion centers of the world, Sara thought. She knew how to dress, even in a foreign place like Texas!

Wrong again. Her slim navy pinstripe with its crisp white collar and belt was just enough off the mark to chafe. Janet wore a jersey dress reminiscent of strawberry sherbet, low necked and clinging, with a marten wrap slung carelessly over one shoulder, and extravagantly high-heeled sandals on her pretty feet. Sara's sober blue pumps mocked every step she took. Brushing at her prim chignon and nervously touching the black jet earrings so at odds with Janet's diamond studs, she dutifully followed them through the restaurant foyer to where Gabe stood chatting with an older woman.

He made the introductions, bid a friendly farewell to the woman, took Sara's hand and complimented her dress. At once suspicious, she thanked him and took back her hand. Just then the headwaiter appeared, greeted Gabe by name, and escorted them to a table for four that was beautifully set with fresh flowers and candles. Gabe seated her with a brush of fingertips down her bare arms, which promptly goosepimpled at his touch. If he noticed the guard she had immediately erected, he gave no sign of it.

"Both the seafood and the steaks are excellent here. If you're in the mood for both, I recommend the filet mignon with a small lobster."

Not knowing what she was in the mood for, Sara decided to accept his advice. Amused, she watched him doing all the manly things necessary to selection of a wine. He caught her curling smile and unabashedly grinned before informing the waiter the wine would do. When she looked terribly impressed by his discriminating judgement, his irrepressible laugh played havoc with her senses.

Throughout the lavish meal, Gabe was urbane, amusing, attentive, and Sara found herself bowled over by such a surfeit of charm and wit. Scarcely knowing what she ate or drank, her spirits rose to the challenge of matching his persuasive charm, and the evening became an unqualified delight.

After the long, leisurely dinner, they went into the small restaurant bar. Sitting cozily around a table barely big enough for two, Gabe casually draped an arm over the back of her chair, his fingertips brushing her shoulder while they chatted with Alex and Janet and listened to the moaning of a cowboy-type singer who seemed to have lost every love he had the ill fortune to encounter.

Sara felt the tearing down of her defenses and by the time they returned to the Regency, she was floating from the combined effects of this attractive man's attentions, and the wine she had consumed. Alex mentioned drinks in his suite, but only Janet accepted. Gabe suavely declined, and Sara felt a distinct sense of being invited to do likewise.

When the two left hand in hand, Sara looked up at Gabe and smilingly thanked him for the evening. Her catch of breath was dismayingly audible as he stepped closer.

"Your key?" he murmured, holding out his hand.

She fished for it for agonizingly long seconds. When at last her fingertips identified the metal object, Sara handed it over and eased aside while he unlocked the door and opened it.

"Goodnight, Gabe," she said too quickly.

"For awhile," Gabe lightly agreed. He touched her nose and walked off.

Sara closed the door and leaned back against it. Her head was none too clear, and it was amazing how vividly his cologne lingered in her nostrils. Was he coming back? Did she want him to? It had been a lovely evening, the kind every woman dreams of.

After a soak in the opulent marble tub, she wrapped up in a bathsheet and dreamily located a nightgown, then impetuously flung it aside in favor of an alabaster robe with delicate lace insets on the fitted bodice. It was after eleven and she felt she ought to go to bed . . . but the soft, cool fabric was a marvelously erotic sensation on her flushed skin. Piling her hair atop her head, she surveyed the results with feminine delight. The sweet-faced woman staring back at her was touched with a gloss of sensuality, an altogether delicious way to look since it perfectly matched her mood.

Making a face at herself, she seemed to float to the enormous bed where she turned back the coverlet. She had just begun to unfasten the buttons on her robe when a soft tap at her door froze her fingers. Genuinely shocked to realize she had been expecting him, and more aware of her femininity than she'd ever been, Sara drifted toward the door and unlocked it.

Gabe had changed to a casual shirt and slacks. A jacket slung over one shoulder, he smiled down at her, taking forever to appraise the shimmering white robe.

"Sara."

It was a sigh, a command, a promise of delights she had never experienced. Vibrantly attuned to every nuance in his voice, she stepped back and closed the door behind him. He draped the jacket over a chair while she stood taut with suspense, his eyes glowing emeralds noting her faintly provocative stance. He came close, looking down at her, a gentle smile curving his mouth. "Sara . . . sweet, sweet Sara," he sighed.

She had not imagined she could literally crave a man's touch. When his hands moved into her hair and begin unpinning it, Sara stood aquiescent, her eyes locked with his as the silken mass came spilling down. Each of his movements was gentle and slow; he slipped his hands deep into her hair and kissed her nose, her cheeks, and each eyelid.

"Sara . . . so fragile and lovely," Gabe said huskily.

Sara closed her eyes as his mouth trailed down her neck to the throbbing hollow of her throat, and slowly moved back up to her yearning lips. She waited in an agony of longing for his mouth to take hers, but the tiny, soft kisses brushed her face until she was trembling with the need to be fiercely, passionately, kissed. The exquisite torment went on and on, playing on her senses with stunning expertise. Even the touch of his lips on her fingertips, one by one while she stood caught in bliss, was an onslaught of practiced seduction.

Giving a deep groan, Gabe suddenly pulled her

against him and took the kiss they both needed. Sara's hands entangled his hair, her lips parting for his ravaging tongue, exulting in the rough caresses bringing her to him until they fused together in tempestuous desire. His long, hard contours of masculinity pressed deeply into her yielding curves, hungrily seeking to get closer. When he swept her up and carried her to the bed, Sara offered no resistance. She wanted him too much to pretend otherwise.

Trustingly she looked up at him as he lay her down, her eyes heavy-lidded with desire. The power of that greedy mouth devouring hers, exploring the sweet wetness with twisting, slanting kisses, drowned out the tiny spark of denial. Gabe unfastened her robe to bare her breasts. When the sable head lowered to her taut, straining nipples, she gasped aloud at the stunning pleasure of a man's rough lips on sensitive flesh. She closed her eyes and moaned softly at the searing caresses, the sweet touch of fire.

He loved her, an inner voice whispered, such depths of tender passion had the power of spoken words! And because she wanted to, needed to, she believed it. When his hand glided to her hips, she turned and arched into him, her own flaring excitement roused to fever pitch by the hard, throbbing urgency of his.

Smoldering green eyes scorched her skin as he raised his head and gazed down upon uptilted breasts and tight little rosebud nipples, a wealth of silky dark hair tumbled over a cream satin pillowsham.

"Gabe, my darling Gabe," Sara said, letting her love flow through his name and her caressing fingertips.

Her liquid voice had an unsettling effect on Gabe. His breathing ragged, he stared at her, his gaze flickering from her parted lips to the expressive eyes gone hazy with unconcealed adoration. She gave him a shy smile and kissed him clingingly.

Gabe abruptly broke the kiss. The odd intensity of his gaze chilled and confused her. "Gabe?" she questioned.

When she tried to kiss him again, Gabe moved aside. Utterly bewildered by his expression, she lay back against the pillow and slowly withdrew her hands from under his collar.

Gabe thrust his fingers through his heavily tousled hair. "Sara, it occurs to me that you haven't had all that many lovers, and that you're putting a little more into this than I bargained for," he said tightly.

Sara twisted around, trying to see his face. "I—I don't understand, Gabe," she said in a stupefied manner.

"That's just the point," he dryly returned. A hand savaged his hair again. "Look, Sara, you're sweet and pretty and desirable, but . . ." Glancing at the all too vulnerable curve of mouth, he grimaced, his voice roughening.

"I thought I made my intentions crystal clear, but just to avoid any chance misunderstanding at some future date, let me lay it out for you. I want you more than I've ever wanted any woman, but that's all there is to it: just wanting, Sara, sex—nothing more. I assumed you knew that love and marriage do not enter into this sort of thing, but I've got a feeling that somewhere in that romantic little head of yours, you're still clinging to some notion that it does. I don't play by those rules, honey," he ended with a cynical smile.

Still aglow with the rapture of lovemaking, Sara shook her head as she tried to make sense of his words. The sardonic tone stabbed her so deeply that it took a hideously long time to assimilate his meaning. When she did, it was a breathtaking blow.

Honey. A pretty word, spoken like an insult. "Are you saying that I planned . . ." she began incredulously. When she looked at him, Gabe was intently watching. "You think I wanted to—to marry you and this was just a . . ." Too stunned to go on, she stared at him in reeling confusion.

"Shrewd female ploy?" Gabe shrugged. "Perhaps. It's been tried on me before, Sara, by far better players than you. After all, it's an old game," he said, turning his face from her.

Sara swallowed hard to curb the surge of nausea. What was wonderful and right an instant ago was suddenly reduced to a sordid act. Shaking with hurt and anger, she sat up and began fastening her gown. His cynical charge was just beginning to sink in with all its vengeful force, and anger flared like a brushfire.

"You egotistical maniac! I hate to deflate such monstrous conceit, but not every woman is hyperventilating at the thought of dragging you to the altar!" she spat.

"Oh? You never had any thoughts in that direction, hum?"

She hated him, hated that thin, twisted smile, the mockery hard in his eyes! A curious iciness enveloped her, a raw, stabilizing force that gave her a moment's respite from hurt. Running a hand down her sleek flank, she tilted her head and smiled.

"Oh, I admit all that money makes you spectacular husband material, but what makes you think I want a husband, Gabe?" she drawled.

Gabe looked so annoyed she knew she had failed. "Sara, let's try to discuss this intelligently? I never meant to hurt you—despite your obvious opinion of me to the contrary. I've always played fair, and I just wanted to make sure you know the score, so you *won't* get hurt."

"Oh for heaven's sake, Gabe! I'm twenty-four years old—of course I know the score! What did you think you had here, a gawky little teenager?" she hotly retorted, sounding, even to herself, precisely that.

"Sometimes I'm not sure exactly what you are," he confessed.

"Well then let me tell you, Gabe! I'm a woman, one who wanted to enjoy the simple physical attraction between myself and a man I hoped could deliver! All I wanted was to—to—"

Unable to carry it further, Sara got off the bed and walked to the bathroom, holding firmly to the rags of her pride. "Oh, goodnight, Gabe—lock the door behind you, please?" she irritably flung over her shoulder.

"Sara, wait!" Gabe said urgently, but she was already in the badly needed sanctuary. Leaning against the door, she bit down on her knuckles to stop the sounds threatening to alert him to the truth. "Sara," he rapped on the door.

"Gabe, just run along? You've already talked it to death. I find if it isn't spontaneous, I don't . . . enjoy it. Now goodnight."

Feeling like a brittle column of glass, she listened intensely for the sound of the door, then shattered in a huddle of weeping. "He loves you—oh yes, doesn't he! You fool, Sara, you stupid fool!" she choked on acrid self-loathing. Would she never stop being such a fool? She made her way to the bed and fell upon it, crying until exhaustion overtook her.

Morning came with a burst of sunshine rather than

the cloudburst she would have preferred. A long, hot shower in no way improved her mood. The day stretched out before her like an unfamiliar obstacle course she had to run without making the slightest error.

Declining Alex's offer of breakfast, she complimented his colorful garb, and shooed him off to dine with Janet, then donned her own elaborate costume. Computing its staggering cost added another knot of tension to the base of her neck. Over four hundred dollars! She didn't have that kind of money to waste on frivolity.

But she would find it, Sara grimly vowed. It was imperative to reimburse Gabe Fielding, even if only to placate a distorted sense of integrity. Dejectedly she looked around the luxurious room. It all seemed so bizarre, as if her life had tilted at a ninety degree angle, and she was still trying to walk upright. She didn't even know who she was anymore, or what she believed in.

Disquieted by the loss of her convictions, Sara got up and checked her handbag for her keys and sunglasses. Gabe would be here shortly. Her mouth twisted as she set Billie's cream-colored Stetson atop her head. It had arrived earlier this morning, cleaned and blocked, brought by a messenger who handed it to her with a cheerful, "Compliments of Mr. Fielding!" That Gabe had taken the trouble to find it and have it restored was perplexing, but she supposed it to be an atonement for his sharp words the day that she had lost it.

His knock jolted her heart. What would they say to one another—how should she act? How would a sophisticated woman behave? She hadn't the faintest idea, Sara admitted. Her panic mounted as he knocked again. Some sophisticate she was—last night's scene scalded her with shame every time it flashed across her mind!

Dreading what she would see in those dangerous green eyes, Sara decided to take her cue from him since she had no prior experience to guide her, and forced her hand to the doorknob.

Chapter Eight

"Hello, Sara," he said, smiling lazily.

Guardedly she met his gaze, but she saw nothing which would give her a clue to his feelings. "Hi, Gabe," she said stiffly. He wore a lustrous white satin shirt boldly accented with black braid, and tailored black trousers which stressed the supple lines of his body. Shamed at how instantly responsive she was to his masculinity, she turned aside and waved him in.

Gabe walked into the room as if he owned it. Tilting his white Stetson at a rakish angle, he observed, "I see you got the hat."

"Oh, yes! It came this morning. Thank you for taking the trouble to find it. I thought it was gone forever," she said. His hand brushed her arm and she recoiled, her eyes clouding as she glanced up at his expressionless face. Was last night to be ignored? She both hoped for, and resented it. How dare he act so normal! Snatching up her purse, she reached for the doorknob. "Well, I guess I'm ready," she said shortly.

"So you are," he smoothly agreed. Flat green eyes moved down her trim figure with deliberate appraisal. "You suppose Alex and Janet are ready? I've got a car waiting downstairs."

Sara laughed with jarring falseness. "I'm sure they are. Alex was here just minutes ago, handsome as a peacock strutting around my room!" She swept out the door with Gabe sauntering along behind her. Looking superbly at ease, he complimented Janet on her silver and green costume, and assured Alex he was born to be a Texan.

As they walked through the lobby, she felt embarrassingly conspicuous, but no one looked askance at their flashy attire. Gabe handed her into the dark gray Cadillac, then expertly guided it through the traffic that jammed every entrance to the Astrodome gleaming in the distance.

Once inside the giant dome, Alex and Janet decided to stay in the skybox which Gabe's firm maintained, but Sara opted for the velvet seats far below. She had never seen a rodeo. Gabe bought her peanuts and popcorn, greasy hot dogs dripping with mustard, icy beer in paper cups and a banner to wave, and it was terribly hard to pretend she wasn't having fun. Little by little she thawed until, her eyes sparkling under the wide brimmed hat, she laughed up at him in open admission of her enjoyment. Last night's humiliation was temporarily shelved in favor of the exciting spirit of rodeo.

But it returned as soon as they were back in the car. Sara tipped her hat over her face and leaned back against the seat with a tired sigh as Gabe guided the Cadillac onto the freeway. They were all subdued, and

Janet suggested a nap before the evening's festivities. Gabe deposited them at the Regency with a reminder that he would pick them up at seven thirty.

Roguish green eyes captured Sara's unwilling gaze. "Have a good rest, Sara. We want you bright-eyed and bushy-tailed for tonight," Gabe mischievously murmured.

Wondering why on earth she persisted in loving this arrogant man, Sara nodded curtly and followed Alex.

Janet's suggestion of a rest seemed eminently sensible. Once in the blessed sanctuary of her room, Sara stripped of the western attire and fell into bed.

Fortunately Alex called to wake her in time to bathe and dress. Abstractedly toweling, powdering and perfuming herself, she donned a flirty little dress of black chiffon that left her back bare to the waist, and danced around her knees in a froth of flippy crystal pleats. She supposed the evening would include dinner and dancing, but what lay at the end of it was painful conjecture. Certainly she had no intentions of repeating any part of last night's scene. It had been her first and last attempts at playing the liberated woman, Sara warned herself. Even a fool knew when to quit.

Ignoring Gabe's knock, she swept her hair to one side and pinned it with a white silk gardenia, while she reviewed the rules she had set for herself. Then, summoning all her composure, Sara put on a smile and opened the door.

Elegant in a white linen shirt and charcoal gray suit cut with a dashing western flair, he folded his arms and returned her smile. Leisurely looking her over, he drawled, "Nice."

"Thank you. You too. Please come in."

His smile evolved into a teasing grin. "You're not sulking about last night, are you?"

She feigned surprise. "Why no—should I be?"

"Well, I thought you might be just a little disappointed," Gabe said with satiric humor. He touched the flower in her hair, then let his knuckles trail down her satiny cheek. "Could be I made a mistake last night, something I don't ordinarily do. In which case, I'm more sorry than you'll ever know."

Sara looked at him searchingly. For an instant she had imagined she heard more in that offhand apology than he intended, but another lazy smile nullified any such illusion.

Taking it at face value, she lifted a slim shoulder. "Since it's inconceivable that you could make a mistake, particularly with a woman, your apology is disqualified for lack of substance. And don't concern yourself with my disappointment. I'm sure a year or two of therapy will repair the damage," she said dryly.

"Um, well, we could try again," Gabe murmured.

She tilted her head and laughed, her heart cracking at his insouciance. "What, and have you beset with another attack of conscience? Therapy in New York costs eighty dollars an hour, Gabe. How much do you think I can afford? By the way, I'm curious as to what gave you the notion I was fantasizing to such an extent," she said glibly.

His eyes hardened. "Well, perhaps I'm just a natural born cynic, but Robert Fielding got a much warmer reception than plain ole Gabe ever did."

Sara turned quickly before he could see her face. "Well, plain ole Gabe did gain a lot of appeal when he became Gabe Fielding. Grant me the virtue of common sense if nothing else. Shall we go? And where are we going?"

"Emile's. It's a nice place," he said indifferently.

Picking up her wrap, Sara glanced at his closed face

and walked out the door. Her words tasted bitter in her mouth, and the evening loomed ahead as an ordeal to be gotten through with as much grace as possible. Determined to make the best of it, she mentally pushed a button labeled, "light and easy," and set the course of conversation.

Alex and Janet were already at the restaurant when they arrived. Sara's dinner was tasteless and her throat ached from forced laughter, but she gave a creditable performance. Several people stopped by their table to greet Gabe and Janet, and it was warmly satisfying to see their pleased recognition of Alex Brandt.

Janet's mood matched his, and it was she who made the impulsive suggestion that they go to Gilley's, the famed country music hall in Pasadena. Gabe cocked an eyebrow with his ironic smile. "Why not? From the sublime to the ridiculous," he murmured, looking around the elegant restaurant. "Are you game?" he asked Sara.

"I guess so. What is Gilley's?"

"I'll let you form your own opinion. Everyone set?" Gabe inquired.

After a trip to the powder room, everyone agreed they were set. As Gabe took her arm to escort her to the car, Sara held herself aloof from his touch. Alex and Janet had their own car, and she dreaded the prospect of what looked to be a very long drive, but Gabe's fascinating tales of Texas eliminated any awkwardness. That he could so totally ignore all that had passed between them amazed her, but at the moment, she was heartily thankful. She expressed her gratitude with such rapt attention and genuine interest that they were in Pasadena before she knew it.

Gilley's was madness, and it was infectious. The enormous barn-like structure was filled with insanely happy people, incredible noise, laughter and excitement. Once they located a table in the cave-like din, Sara agreed to a gin and tonic, and turned to watch the action on the immense dance floor. The air throbbed with the beat of loud, wailing music. Gabe sat disturbingly close, and when she leaned to hear what he said, his clean-shaven cheek touched hers.

After a scant half hour, Alex turned to Janet and said, "I think I've soaked up enough atmosphere. What say you and I leave the children to enjoy this madness, and find us a place with very soft music and a waiter hovering at my elbow with a pitcher of very dry martinis?"

Sara panicked as Janet promptly stood up in agreement; being left with Gabe was a paralyzing thought! However, Gabe intended to stay, and she was too flustered to alter the situation. As Alex's comforting bulk disappeared in the crowd, Sara felt horribly ill at ease, but Gabe leaned back in his chair and smilingly suggested another drink, to which she nervously agreed.

The silence yawned between them. Unwittingly she began keeping time to the pulsating beat of music, feeling a wildness building up, a violent need to vent her inner turbulence. She shivered as his hand curved over her shoulder.

"Want to try that?" he murmured, gesturing to the dance floor.

"Try it! I don't even know what it is," Sara protested.

Gabe stood up. "That's called the Cotton-eyed Joe." He laughed down at her as she gave the dance dubious regard. "It's possible even a New Yorker could do it," he taunted.

"At least a New Yorker will try!" Sara flashed.

Her spirits soared with the hilarity around them as she stumbled through the dance, trying to follow Gabe's instructions. It was fast and furious fun, and by the time it ended, she was flushed with excitement. The band immediately swung into a slow, sensuous rhythm. Gabe caught her arm and drew her back to him, holding her tightly against his hard male thighs. The warm, musky smell of him engulfed her senses. When both his hands moved down to her waist, Sara wound her arms around his neck and gave in to her heart's longing.

She couldn't resist him. Dance after dance, he held her so tightly in his arms that she could feel the charged excitement in the hard, demanding press of his muscular arms. Their eyes locked in erotic combat and he laughed, low and delighted at her provocative challenge. Passion flared between them like blue-flamed electricity.

As they left Gilley's, the cold night air brought her down to earth with a jarring thud. Sara did not attempt conversation; the transition from fantasy to reality left her bereft of pretense. Knowing she was transparently vulnerable, she cuddled into the velvet seat and kept her distance.

"Are you warm enough?" Gabe asked, noting her shiver.

Sara quickly forestalled his obvious intent. The dark intimacy of the car was disturbing enough without having him near. "Yes, I'm fine," she said, but another shiver rippled through her in blatant denial of her assurance. It was an inner chill and had nothing to do with the temperature.

Her arms crossed tightly in front of her, Sara tried to laugh. "A few weeks on the island certainly leaves you susceptible to cold weather! I'll probably freeze to

death when I go back to New York, we have such
terrible winters. Oh, Gabe, don't—"

His mouth was warm and hard on hers, his hands
slipping under her light wrap to pull her into his arms.
Helplessly responsive, she could only cling to him and
thrill to his urgency. Minutes later, he buried his face in
her hair and held her crushingly tight.

"I couldn't wait until we got back to the hotel for
that—I needed it now," he said, seductively soft.

"Gabe . . ." Nothing else would come out, and even
that was a tremulous whisper. Laughing gently, Gabe
kissed her nose, then started the car. When he captured
her hand, he commented on its coldness. How could he
know she was trembling inside? Sara laughed briefly
and blamed the chilly weather again.

Gabe seemed to have taken it for granted that they
would take up where they left off the night before!
Wishing she had the sophistication to handle the situation, Sara was wretchedly aware that she did not. The
drive back to Houston was excruciatingly long. He
made conversation and she laughed in all the right
places, but her mind was a jumble of confusion. She
had never felt so hopelessly out of control.

As the miles passed in tortuously slow succession, his
arrogant assumption began to gall until the saving grace
of anger reminded her that she had a mind of her own.
Mortified by her submission to that dominant male
mastery, she reclaimed her hand for the rest of the trip.

Her splendid wave of outrage got her as far as her
door. Resolving to dismiss him as graciously and as
quickly as possible, Sara dug blindly in her purse for the
key. When she finally located it, Gabe opened the
door, and followed her inside before she could protest.
He locked it behind him, then removed his jacket and
tie.

Blazing at his presumptuous assurance, Sara placed a hand on her hip and regarded him with icy amusement. "Gabe, I admit I've had a few drinks, but not enough to cloud my memory. I don't recall inviting you to stay—I don't even recall asking you in, for that matter. Now if you don't mind, it's late, and I'm exhausted."

The pleasant cast of features flowed into the cold, angry mask she had seen the day that Alana had bolted. With slow, deliberate movements, Gabe pulled off the tie and unbuttoned his collar. "But I do mind, Sara," he said mockingly. "You've been driving me crazy all evening, and I fully intend to accept what you were offering."

"I offered nothing—" *Not what you think—it was love I offered,* Sara's heart wailed.

"The devil you didn't! You came on to me tonight and I'll be damned if you're backing out!" Gabe caught her shoulders in a tight, painful grip. "I told you once, Sara, if you started something you'd better be prepared to carry through. I want you and I'm damn well going to have you," he said with steely softness.

"We seem to have a problem communicating, Gabe. You see, I don't want you."

Gabe swore at her sweetly given insult. A hand entangled her hair with a rough grip, and his mouth came down in a deep kiss. The arm holding her against him tightened when she struggled. His body moving intimately against hers, he forced her back to the wall and ran his hands over her in rough possession.

Sara fought a hopelessly divided battle. His body effortlessly held her pinned to the wall while he devoured her with his hands and mouth and the heat of glittering green eyes on fire with her resistance. Stunned by her reaction to this primitive male passion, she swayed when he loosened the pressure. Even while some small part of her screamed its outrage, she felt wild with the need to continue this blazingly exciting lovemaking.

His ravenous mouth dropped to her throat, kissing, nibbling—deliciously sharp little nips that thrilled and aroused her. When he caught her lips again with hungered urgency, the explosive combination of love and desire overwhelmed Sara. Gabe wrapped her achingly tight, and reality became only the volcanic excitement surging from his body to hers.

Gabe's deep groan added fuel to the flames within her. His tongue made a ravishing foray through the honey of her mouth, his hands greedily exploring the supple curves tantalizing his maleness. Aroused to a fever pitch, Sara instinctively moved to the delight of hard-muscled thighs straining against heated softness. Her tongue entangled his in a hot, wild duel of desire.

"Let's go to bed now, Sara. I've waited long enough," Gabe said thickly.

A pathetic shred of pride made her shake her head in denial of that arrogant demand.

"Sara!"

Sara looked up at him in dazed reaction to the flat, hard warning. "No, I said . . . I don't want . . ." Holding herself in rigid check, she shoved at his chest. His clasp tightened. Her hand swung out in a furious arc which he caught before it made contact with his face.

"Oh no, Sara, I let you get away with it once, but I won't take it again!" he grated. "Now we're going to bed—"

Engulfed in a maelstrom of pain and fury, Sara struck out blindly, spitting shockingly ugly words to confirm his suspicions.

"We're going nowhere—not until you know exactly what I want! Let me lay it out for you, Gabe, so there

won't be any future misunderstandings!" she mocked.
"I'll go to bed with you, but not for pleasure—not just
to satisfy crude physical attraction! I play for keeps,
Robert, and I have no intention of losing my head to
that irresistible charm of yours! Unless there's something on the bottom line, your charm wears thin in a
hurry!"

Sickened by her dreadful lie, Sara cringed at his
reaction. His lips thinned to a shapeless line, and a cold
white anger set his features into unyielding granite as
he studied her. His fingers tightened until she gasped.

"However, I can hardly deny that in this situation,
brute strength dominates," she said scathingly.

Gabe began to laugh. Unable to disguise her confusion, Sara stared at him, her bruised mouth a circle of
surprise.

"I've never yet resorted to brute strength, Sara.
Most women consider it an honor to share my bed," he
drawled with a look of utter arrogance. Hard green
eyes raked the lovely dress, and an insolent shrug drove
the knife deeper. "The situation, as you call it, hardly
merits such excessive effort on my part."

Gabe dropped his hands with a contemptuous smile.
"Your game is not only passé, Sara, but rather boring
to a man. If it didn't work in New York, why did you
think it would in Texas?" he asked.

"I didn't . . . in New York, I don't . . ." she shook
her head.

"Ah, I see. No prospects worth the effort in New
York, hum?"

This cold-eyed stranger was so far removed from the
gentle, teasing Gabe she loved, Sara's face openly
registered her bewilderment. The clinging mist of
shame and revulsion totally stripped her of defenses.
She gave a deep shudder, and turned away.

"As you said, nobody is worth the effort. Please leave me alone, Gabe, I'm very tired. Just go now?" she said dully. She lowered her head and her hair veiled her face like a dark raincloud. "Oh, by the way, I found out what those ridiculous clothes cost you, and I'll send you a check for it first thing next week," she added in a stronger voice. Sensing his impatient movement, she walked across the room, wiping furtively at her tears.

"Don't be even more ridiculous, Sara!" Gabe snarled. When he touched her arm, she recoiled. Furiously he jerked her around to face him.

Pain and mistrust darkened her eyes. "I don't think I'm being ridiculous in refusing to accept clothing from a total stranger. I was brought up that way, you see; flowers, perfume, candy are the only acceptable gifts from men you don't know," she said wryly. A bitter smile etched her lips. "Not by choice, of course, just part of the game."

"Damn you!" Gabe said, his voice low and savage. "Looking at me with those eyes like bruised flowers . . ." A strange look washed over his face, a sadness mingled with contempt and pain and weary disgust. It was a look so complex that Sara was unsure what she was seeing.

He shook his head sharply. "I fancy myself a perceptive man, but you really had me fooled. What I mistook for clean, fresh innocence was only cunning self-interest. You're as shrewd and calculating as any woman born."

Sara shrugged. "I prefer to call it a natural sense of self-preservation. And don't look so righteous, Gabe," she chided acidly. "We were both after something a little less than noble, wouldn't you agree?"

He laughed, relaxing into amusement. "Yes, I guess we were. Pursuing our natural instincts, hum, Sara?"

Too transparent to withstand the scrutiny of his cynical green eyes, Sara turned aside. "Something like that. Goodnight, Gabe," she said tiredly.

"Goodnight. Sleep well, Sara," he mockingly returned. Grabbing his jacket and tie, Gabe strode out the door.

Sara locked it behind him, then collapsed on the couch to cry out her bitter anguish. Eventually she fell asleep there, and awoke with a painful crick in her neck.

Blinking at the brilliant stream of sunlight that had fallen on her face, she sat up and held her aching head as last night's nightmare began assuming tangible shape and form. "Oh, Gabe, it was a lie—it was all a lie!" she whispered wretchedly. Tearing off her clothing, she stumbled to the bathroom and stepped into the hot, cleansing water.

Wrapped in a towel and clouds of rejuvenating steam, Sara emerged rosy-skinned to check the time. Eight-thirty. Alex had suggested breakfast at nine in the hotel restaurant, she remembered. Anxiously she examined her face. Except for her reddened eyelids, she looked much healthier than she felt.

Two nights in a row she had wept for Gabe Fielding. *No more.*

Since they were touring Houston today, she dressed for comfort in a shimmering red-wine velour pullover, dark gray slacks and suede flats. She took two aspirin, then nestled into the velvet chair for some urgent calculations.

The money she owed Gabe was an acid lump in her stomach. She could borrow it from Alex, but even the thought made her wince. Yet there was no possible way she could pay it back on her own. The weeks of paychecks she had received on the island had already been signed over to the nursing home which had cared for her father during his extensive illness, and at the moment, she had approximately thirty-eight dollars in the bank.

"*Approximately* three hundred and eighty bucks short," Sara muttered. Despite her handsome salary, spendthrift Billie was probably as strapped as she, and there was no one else close enough to turn to. But owing Gabe Fielding a dime was simply untenable!

At last the solution presented itself with painful simplicity. Before Billie had achieved her current success as a model, she spent several years existing on small, sporadic paychecks, and had more than once used the temporary services of a pawnshop to keep afloat. Sara promptly placed a call to New York.

"Billie? Hello love, it's Sara! Now listen, I'm calling from Houston and I . . . oh, Billie!" Sara groaned as her words unleashed a fusillade of excited questions. "Billie, I promise to write and tell you everything, every single detail, but right now I am calling long distance, so just please listen?"

Hurriedly she explained her need for money and Billie's part in obtaining it. She was to take the jewelry left to Sara by her parents and pawn it. "Just do it, Billie, and deposit whatever you get to my account, then call me immediately? Yes, it's that urgent," Sara said tiredly.

A few minutes later, she managed to end the call and slowly replaced the receiver. As was usual when she found herself doing something she knew to be stupid, she was scratching her left wrist raw.

Sara glanced at her watch. After nine, too late to join Alex for breakfast. She wasn't hungry anyway. Billie had been discouraging about the value of her jewelry. If she got half of what she needed, she could count herself lucky.

There were angry red scratches on her wrist. "Oh blast," Sara whispered, wiping at her eyes. The thick, plush carpet cushioning her feet was a bitter reminder of another's wealth. What would a paltry four hundred dollars mean to Gabe Fielding! He had probably spent that much on dinner and drinks last night.

None of which mattered, she told herself firmly. Just as she stood up to wash her face, the telephone rang. "Sara? Good morning," Gabe said crisply. "I've spoken with Alex, and we're meeting in the lobby in ten minutes."

"Yes, ten minutes," she agreed, and hung up.

Sinking back into the chair, Sara sat staring blankly at the wall. How on earth could she face him! She had deliberately gone along with his assumption that she was interested in his money—when the Gabe she loved hadn't a spare dime! It seemed incredible that Sara Tracey, usually the most forthright and candid of persons, could have willfully woven this web of deception around herself and the man she loved.

The deep generosity of her nature held herself entirely to blame for her misery. She had behaved in a stupid, even uncivilized manner for which there was no acceptable excuse. The sin of pride, she thought contritely. A few honest words would have prevented this intolerable situation, and yet, even now, gifted with the usual profound hindsight, no clarifying words occurred to her. What could she have said? "I love you, Gabe"? Wasn't that just what he sensed, and rejected to the point of interrupting their lovemaking? How would he react to an actual declaration of love? Pained annoyance, or sardonic disbelief? There was no in between;

150

Sara was convinced it would have been one or the other.

There was, of course, the matter of why he had formed such an unflattering impression in the first place. She supposed her devious attempt to play the flippant, worldly woman had done the trick. Stupidity piled on stupidity, and all of it hers. Well, at least she knew exactly where she stood with him. No more clinging to hope against all reason—she was finally cured of her foolish illusions. Since his interest in her was purely sexual, she could think of no cause for expending further energy on futile attempts to alter his opinion. Let him think what he would; she would neither confirm nor deny it. Knowing how cheaply he valued their friendship, it seemed the sensible course to follow.

What had he called her? Shrewd and calculating. Sara was overcome with bitter laughter—if only he knew the truth! She was about as shrewd as a dormouse and very nearly as intelligent.

Chapter Nine

Sara stood in the sunny kitchen preparing a dinner tray of savory pot roast and the spice cake she had baked earlier. Shortly after their return to the island, Alex had contracted the measles, complicated by bronchitis, and the vastly outraged convalescent made her life as miserable as he felt. Since she had already had measles and Elena had not, Sara took over the cooking and cleaning in the maid's absence. She would have enjoyed it had not Alex's wounded-buffalo roars continually reverberated throughout the house.

Absently, she completed the tray, her mind still on the man she had not seen since Houston nearly three weeks ago. He had called several times to check on Alex, but she could think of nothing to say to Gabe, and apparently he had nothing to say to her; after a brief exchange of amenities, she had summoned Alex to the telephone.

Sara shivered, recalling that last interminable day in

Houston. They had been two casual acquaintances, concealing a host of bitter words under cool, impersonal, achingly polite smiles and proper comments. Their parting words, conducted in the cheery presence of Alex and Janet, still had the power to stab her heart. After warmly bidding Alex goodbye, Gabe had turned to her with a glint of cold humor lighting his hard green eyes.

"It's been my particular pleasure introducing you to Houston, Sara. Perhaps we can do it again sometime. Take care now."

Imagining she saw the contempt she felt for herself in that flat green gaze, Sara had been compelled to retaliate. "You too, Gabe. This has been the most instructive weekend of my life—I can't begin to thank you," she sweetly assured him.

"You give it far more importance than it merits, believe me, Sara," Gabe had protested.

Perhaps she did, Sara agreed, then, and now. Anxiously she wondered if he had received her check. He had not mentioned it, and she hadn't the nerve to ask. Two days after returning to Isla de Paz, Billie had called her with good news. She had met a lovely man named Glen who had tons of money and the good sense to fall madly in love with Billie. Naturally he had been delighted to hold Sara's jewelry as security against a four hundred dollar loan—as a favor to Billie, of course. The money had been deposited in Sara's New York account, and she in turn promptly sent Gabe a check.

More good news subsequently arrived from Billie. She had decided to marry the wise and wealthy Glen and settle down to have babies, so Sara wasn't to worry about her jewelry—she would have simply ages to redeem it.

The sag went out of Sara's shoulders at that last part. She would eventually redeem her parents' jewelry and erase the shame of having gotten herself into a situation requiring such an ignominious sacrifice. As soon as they returned to New York, she would take a second job in the evening, and this second income would be reserved strictly for that very honorable debt.

Having so resolved, Sara's heart was immensely lightened, at least concerning this situation. Gabe was another matter, one over which she had no control.

Alex moodily wandered into the kitchen and elected to eat at the table rather than in the abominable bedroom. With sweet patience, Sara bore his complaints about the meal, the quality of the sunlight, and the state of the world in general. Alex had never been sick a day in his life, and his indignation knew no bounds.

The book was not going well; he had, in his own melodramatic words, gone dry. Sensing his very real frustration, Sara was careful to conceal her amusement, and kept her voice matter-of-fact as they discussed his tragic disabilities. Once he returned to his room, she cleaned the kitchen, then bathed and dressed. Too restless to read, she roamed through the silent house, remembering Houston, the rapture of love, the anguish of seeing her reflection in those contemptuous green eyes.

What was the point of going over it again! Angrily she swept open the terrace door and stepped out into the shadowed hush, found a lawn chair, curled up and closed her eyes. Given Alex's genuine frustration, she had a feeling they would not remain there much longer. Such soft, luxurious living had an insidious way of undermining a disciplined will, as she well knew. Alex needed the taut excitement of a more challenging atmosphere: New York in all its noisy, crowded, glittering glory. But she would stay here forever if she had the choice. She loved every inch of the clean, beautiful island.

She gave a violent start as a deep, resonant voice filled the darkness. "Good evening, Sara," Gabe said. An instant later he had snapped on the lights and was standing over her.

Blinking, Sara stared at him. For a frightening moment, he was a stranger, his face grim and dark and menacing, and then he smiled, stepping nearer, his manner no longer threatening. Yet behind that ironic smile she sensed anger and tension, a dark whisper of violence held in tight restraint. Her heart beating too fast for comfort, she returned his greeting. As she got to her feet, he jammed a hand into his shirt pocket and pulled out her check.

"Would you mind telling me what this is?"

"Why, my check, of course. I told you I was reimbursing you. It's a simple matter of paying off a debt . . ." Sara faltered at the blaze of fury firing his eyes.

"A simple matter of paying off a debt? *It's an insult and you know it!*"

She stared at him in astonishment. "Please, lower your voice. Alex is asleep. And I never meant it to be an insult." Honestly confused by his anger, she touched his arm. "Gabe, really, I think you're being unreasonable—"

"Unreasonable? Sara, I have entertained everything from a princess to a grand duchess, and not once has anyone thrown my hospitality back in my face!" he said fiercely.

Looking down at the pale oval face delicately framed by wispy black curls, even Gabe was baffled at the extent of his anger. Sara wore a loose blue shift that wrapped gently about her slender figure, alternately revealing and concealing her unbound breasts and the gentle curves of her hips. Savagely he thrust a hand through his hair. When he spoke again, his voice leveled off to a sardonic drawl.

"What was this defiant little gesture supposed to prove, Sara?"

Sara's temper flashed in her eyes, but she was determined to avoid another ugly scene. She had enough stupidity to her credit; there was no need to add to the list! "It's not a gesture of defiance, it's simply a matter of personal policy, that's all," she stated quietly. "Gabe, I'm really sorry my check upset you, but the matter stands; I will not owe anyone, and particularly not you." Cool and remote, she tipped her chin and stared him down.

Gabe's harsh laugh registered only as a wince of pain in her somber blue eyes. As he pulled her into his arms and sought to kiss her, Sara turned her face and stood rigid in his embrace, refusing to dignify him with any kind of response. She felt him stiffen, heard his swiftly indrawn breath, and knew she was aching to give him the response he wanted, and would give him, if she had to bear this sweet torment a second longer.

When his grip relaxed, she looked up at him and said, "If you don't mind, I prefer to end this right now. I'm not in the mood to be mauled tonight."

The taut silence was shattered by his cynical laugh. "Okay, Sara, whatever you say. It's a matter of supreme indifference to me. However, I can't accept your check; that's a personal policy of *mine*." His mocking drawl was suddenly edged with anger. "When I give a woman anything—even a lousy shirt and a pair of boots—I don't expect to have my generosity repaid by insult!"

A little amused at his theatrical gesture, Sara watched as he ripped the check to pieces and cast them to the ground. She gave an eloquent shrug. "That was a childish thing to do. You ought to know me well enough by now to realize I'll simply write you another. And another, ad infinitum, if need be. Now please go. I've worked hard all day, and I'm too tired for this nonsense. Goodnight."

How she made it through the next few days, Sara would never know. She was in limbo, a gray, shadowy place without an echo. Alex was soon up and about, fully recovered and as restive as a caged animal. Even Janet's visits did little to lessen his gnawing frustration. He couldn't write. It was as simple as that, and such simplicity had the power to shake the earth, or at least this small part of it, thought Sara.

She sighed at the prospect of another long afternoon by herself. Listlessly she changed into a bikini and terry cloth jacket, filled a thermos with limeade, and struck out on foot for the woodland pool. She had not been on a horse since her return from Houston, another subtle denial of any taint of charity, she vaguely supposed. At any rate, she had no desire to go near the stables.

The pool glowed darkly under its overhanging canopy of leaves, but the irregular circle of sunlight in the center glowed a sparkling, pellucid green, discomfitingly reminiscent of Gabe's eyes the last time she saw him. How angry he had been that night, and over something as frivolous as a four hundred dollar check! She supposed she had somehow humiliated him, pricked that immense and arrogant pride. True to her word, she had promptly sent off another check, but what he would do with it was left to conjecture.

The slippery black stone ledge felt satiny smooth and cool against her skin. Enjoying it, she stretched her legs full length in the water, perversely recalling the first time she had met Gabe there, when he had been just Gabe. Achingly she wished she could turn back time and reclaim that relationship. She had loved him long before she knew who he was.

A prickling sensation along her spine brought her swiftly to her feet. Sara gasped aloud as she saw him leaning indolently against a tree, watching her with that lack of expression she had come to loathe.

"Hi, Gabe," she called as she splashed to shore. He moved quickly to assist her, retaining her hands when he stood beside her.

"What happened to your finger?" he curtly inquired, examining a rather elaborate bandage Alex had concocted in lieu of a simple band-aid.

"Oh, I cut myself. What are you doing here, spying on me like that?" she asked sharply. Pulling her hands free, she walked up on the bank and picked up her towel. Whether or not he followed was immaterial to her, Sara thought hotly. He was dressed in those shabby jeans and sneakers again, and this fired her anger. Unconsciously provocative, she dried her sun-kissed body, then began brushing her hair, too occupied to look up, nonetheless very aware of his presence. If only her heart would stop this jarring thud!

"Are you on foot?" he idly asked.

"Yes," she said shortly.

"Skeet tells me you haven't been near the stables since you got back. Another gesture of defiance?"

Flushing, she tipped her chin. "Don't be absurd.

Riding is no longer a pleasure, that's all. Besides, I've been too busy playing housekeeper and cook." A winsome smile crinkled her eyes. "Actually, I loved it," she confessed. "It's a lovely house. I'm going to miss it—"

"Miss it?" Gabe interrupted sharply.

"Yes, we'll be leaving soon, I expect."

"No one said anything to me about leaving. Alex didn't mention it."

"Perhaps he didn't know he needed your permission to leave . . ." She shrugged. "At any rate, we are leaving."

Gabe broke a twig with a sharp snap of sound and tossed it in the water, then picked up another and began destroying it with vicious force. What was he so angry about now? Sara wondered uneasily. Feeling intensely awkward, she flung down the brush and raked her fingers through her hair, tossing it back with provocative hauteur.

Gabe hurled the shredded twig into the water. "Okay, Sara, I cede the victory. Will you marry me?"

Sara's shock was so absolute, she was incapable of answering for a horribly long interval. Enormous blue circles of disbelief turned up to his inscrutable gaze. *Marry you!*

"Yes."

"But I don't understand—"

"I think you do," Gabe said, his tone dark with mockery.

Sara's voice steadied. "Are you making some kind of joke, Gabe? Because if you are, I don't find it amusing, or even in good taste."

A fleeting smile twisted his lips. "No joke, Sara," he said evenly.

"But—but *why?*"

"Because I want you in my bed and that seems to be the only way of getting you now," he said ironically. Hungrily his gaze moved over her breasts, the roundness of hips openly displayed by her brief suit until Sara felt naked. "I never thought I'd want anything so badly, but I do." He shrugged. "I'm a businessman, so I'll pay whatever the price."

Sara's mouth worked, but nothing came out. He couldn't be serious—even a man who regarded marriage as a commercial enterprise couldn't be this callous!

When she located her voice, it was choked with pain. "I have never heard anything so arrogant, so cold-blooded and—and ugly in my life!" she cried passionately. "What about love, caring, commitment—sharing—"

"Well, we'll be sharing a bed," Gabe coolly returned. "Since you want it as much as I do, that should suffice—for awhile, anyway."

"For . . . awhile?" she dumbly repeated.

He laughed mirthlessly. "Well, who knows how long I'll desire you. Maybe you have long-lasting qualities, maybe not. At least we'll find out, won't we?"

His voice roughened as she raised a trembling hand to her mouth. "Sara, it's simply a business proposition. Wanting you has become a ridiculous obsession, one I despise, but I can't rid myself of it. So I'll marry you. Naturally I'll expect you to sign a waiver of some sort—I have no intention of giving you half of the Fielding assets, but we'll work out an equitable settlement which will cover any contingency. In other matters, we'll both respect the other's rights, including the privilege of complete and separate privacy."

"Privacy?" she echoed blankly.

"Yes. We're each free to do as we please, when we please. In fact, we'll sit down together and draft a bill of rights just so . . ." His voice grew savagely mocking. "Just so there'll be no future misunderstandings concerning our individual pleasures."

Sara was staggered by what he implied. "You mean we'd . . . you'd see other women?" she asked incredulously.

"Fidelity is not part of the bargain, Sara," he said cruelly. "My life is perfectly balanced—or will be, once I'm sane again, and I'll tolerate no disruptive scenes on what I can or cannot do. In other words, I will enjoy other women when and if I please—with discretion, of course." He smiled. "Naturally, I'll extend the same privilege to you."

Unable to believe what she was hearing, Sara stared at him, and then hit him so hard that he staggered backwards.

Her heart stopped as rage suffused his face; the big, powerful hands clenching with white-knuckled force. "Oh, Gabe, I'm sorry, I—please, please go away and leave me alone!" she implored. Helpless to stem the tears raining down her cheeks, she turned blindly and groped for a towel.

Gabe grabbed her shoulders and swung her around, shaking her, looking as if he'd like to strangle her —looking capable of it! "What are you crying about— you got what you wanted, didn't you?" he ground out.

Desperately she searched his dark, contemptuous face, and knew it to be hopeless, but she had to try. "No, I didn't get what I wanted. I don't want to marry you for your money—I don't give a fig for all your wealth! That night in Houston—Gabe, I only reacted that stupid way because—because I was ashamed at

161

being so unsophisticated. You were right, you see, I haven't had all that many lovers and I didn't know how to handle it, I—"

She stopped and lowered her face, her hair veiling her face. What was the point in telling him she'd had no lovers? He would only find it amusing.

She raised her wet blue eyes slowly to his, her voice hardening. "At any rate, when I marry it will be for totally irrational reasons, like love and mutual respect and until death do us part, so I'll have to decline the . . . honor of being your wife, even on a trial basis," she said, her smile as bitter as her tone.

Gabe's low, savage curse was a chilling explosion of sound as he reached for her. At first Sara was too stunned to react, then a surge of revulsion broke her paralysis and she began to struggle, twisting her face from his brutally searching mouth, hating him and fighting with wildcat fury. He laughed deeply, his fingers tightening on her soft upper arms as he held her with rough enjoyment in the desperately uneven battle. Sara freed a hand and struck him across the face, and would have done so again, but he caught her wrist and twisted it behind her back.

"Let go of me, you—! I loathe you—I can't stand for you to touch me!" she hissed, panting with rage as he held her with contemptuous ease.

"Can't you, Sara?" he taunted. And then his mouth found hers, hard and demanding, bruising her lips as his hands dug deep and pressed her against him. His dark, explosive excitement aroused a corresponding passion. Sara fought all the more, a twisting, squirming fury held in a grip of steel, kissed again and again with ruthless mastery while she hammered on his shoulders —and her lips became soft and clinging.

Her legs weakened from his relentless assault on her senses, and she was remotely surprised to find herself lying in the sweet-smelling grass. Gabe came down on top of her, a heavy, familiar weight to which her body instantly responded. Weakly she resisted the desire flaming through her. His hands moved over her with roughly tender urgency, caressing with fevered delight as his mouth drank deep of her sweetness. His searching fingers thrust beneath her tiny bikini trunks to find her naked warmth and strain her hips to his.

When her arms suddenly wound around him, Gabe kissed her with blazing passion. The ardent response he hungered for was suddenly, sweetly his, a shout of exultance in his blood. "Sara, Sara, don't you know I'd give anything—*anything*—to have this?" he muttered hoarsely.

The words were a shock of icy water. An obsession, he had said, one he despised. How could she have forgotten! Utterly drained of desire, Sara dropped her arms and lay inert as his mouth roamed her face and neck with burning kisses. The hard thud of his heart slammed her breasts, mocking the frantic beat of her own. A profound sadness moved deep within her. It was the strangest feeling, she thought dully, exactly like being numbed by an icy anesthetic.

She was suddenly sick to death of it all. "So have it, Gabe, and let's be done with it. Take it if you want it—I give you freely the very dubious honor of being my first lover. I couldn't care less," she said tonelessly.

She felt his body grow rigid at her words. Sara laughed aloud, a bitter, metallic sound. "You would have had it anyway, had you only been patient. The Gabe who took me for a lovely moonlight ride on a golden stallion, who laughed and kissed and teased me, made me feel pretty and special . . . if I could only have known him a little longer, I would have given him anything. I liked and trusted him . . ."

Sara looked him squarely in the eye. "I neither like nor trust Robert Fielding. In fact, I despise him."

The silence seemed to last a small forever. Sara heard a plane far away, and the sweet, piercing song of a bird nearby; she heard the groaning breath Gabe took. She felt detached, remote, unable to care what he did.

Gabe rolled away from her and sat up. His hands caught his face, savagely rubbing as he vented a half strangled laugh. "Sara, there have been times when the convoluted logic of a female mind utterly baffles me. This is one of those times . . . There have also been times when I devoutly wished I had never met a woman named Sara Lynne Tracey, and this is another."

"That makes two of us," Sara said flatly.

He got to his feet and stood staring down at her with an odd hunger in his eyes. Not passion, not even obsession; what was it, she wondered. Whatever it was, she ached to console it. That's stupid—I hate him! Sara thought, fighting a hysterical laugh.

Glancing around the lovely woodland pool, Gabe massaged the back of his neck. "I apologize for this—and for every time I kissed you. I apologize for buying you clothing and offering you marriage. I apologize for seeing you that first time and telling Skeet to give you Alana—I apologize to *hell* and back, and if that doesn't do it, I'm damned sorry!" They stared at one another, a long, stinging look of mutual bitterness.

Gabe's mouth twisted into a hurt, wry smile. "It's just possible that the Gabe you first met and Robert Fielding are one and the same, you know. But rest assured that neither of them will bother you again."

With that, he turned and strode swifty through the trees.

Alone. The word seemed to throb with every beat of her heart as Sara walked the remaining distance to a house she had come to love. *And would soon be leaving, never to return again.*

During the following week, she moved through a peculiarly colorless vacuum, somewhat akin to watching a blurred black and white film splotched with garish incidents of color. The night she went to Gabe's house was one such incident. Driven by the sheer desperation of knowing she loved him, would always love him, could not leave the island without making a stab at preserving a very precious thing, she had gone to him—

And discovered the utter futility of honest intent. Gabe and Moneta were on the terrace, one silhouette in the moonlight. Moneta's hair gleamed like hoarfrost against the dark head she was drawing to hers.

It had been pain slashing at her until Sara felt torn to shreds by its claws. She left without disturbing them. Yet, despite her anguish, she felt curiously at peace with herself as she faced a solid truth. It was over and done with.

Attending to the packing and the hundred little details that accompany a move kept her occupied past the point of thinking. She enjoyed nothing; the island itself had become anathema, and Sara could not wait to leave it. She wished with all her heart that they had not parted in such bitterness, but there was nothing she could do about that. She would not, under any circumstances, see Gabe again.

Only when she saw his plane landing or taking off did her bitter resolve begin to fray at the edges. Gabe made no attempt to make contact, and she ached with memories which had no substance. She told herself it was stupid to remember only the fun they'd had together, the times of laughter and sweet, warm rapport, the dusky evening she had met a man of rare quality and took his hand to walk beside him.

"Well, that about finishes it, huh, Sara!" Alex gloated when they packed the last box.

"Yes, Alex, it's finished," Sara said.

On a bright Sunday morning they left Isla de Paz, their mode of travel a gleaming white yacht that belonged to one of Janet's friends. As Alex strolled off to join them, Sara leaned against the rail, fixing her gaze on the familiar island fast becoming a dark green lump in the turquoise sea. It had been an experience she would always remember. Relegating its importance to this sentimental thought reduced the pain to manageable proportions. Grief was merely a compact knot which could now be tucked into a distant corner of her heart until it faded, as she was sure it would, just as the image of this lovely island would in time dim to a misty memory.

Gazing at the pretty green cutout that was Isla de Paz, as insubstantial as moonlight and fairy tales, Sara was frozen to utter stillness as a blue and silver plane lifted into the air like an exotic bird. It circled the island in lazy farewell, then turned in a direction opposite the yacht.

"*Vaya con Dios,* my love," she whispered, watching the plane shrink to a silvery speck.

In a moment it was gone, and the sky was as empty as the sea.

Chapter Ten

Concealed behind huge wraparound sunglasses, Sara spilled out of the subway with the rest of the weary throng, and walked rapidly to her apartment. After the peace and tranquillity of Isla de Paz, the city seemed incredibly clamorous. She had been home three weeks now, but she was still overwhelmed by the smells and sounds and sense of being smothered by crowds.

She hadn't yet gotten used to living alone, either, she thought as she opened the door of the dark, empty apartment. Just hours before Sara had returned to New York, Billie had eloped with her wealthy admirer and was currently on a honeymoon which seemed destined to cover the entire Caribbean and a good part of the Pacific, and there had been only a hastily scrawled note on the kitchen table to welcome Sara home. Envious thoughts were inevitable, and the pain they engendered tainted the joy she earnestly tried to feel for Billie's radiant happiness, which was so evident in every post-card she had dashed off from glamorous places.

Glancing at her watch, Sara saw she had an hour before reporting for work at the café. She fixed herself a glass of iced tea, then took down the yellow canister which held the cash earmarked for Billie's husband. Three weeks of waitressing made a depressingly small pile of wrinkled bills. Tips were either negligible or non-existent; she should have tried for one of those expensive restaurants, she supposed. But this one was nearby, the hours were perfectly suited to her schedule, and walking two blocks at midnight was infinitely more desirable than an hour on a crosstown bus.

She replaced the money and set the canister back on the shelf. Thank goodness Alex had no inkling of her extra activities. If she felt tired in the mornings, she never betrayed it. Work was an anodyne, and she enjoyed her hectic schedule. With so few free moments, she was less vulnerable to idle thoughts which invariably drifted back to Gabe and Isla de Paz.

The sunlight dusting her windows had a muddy look, not at all like the clear, golden light of the island. It had had a luminous quality, she recalled, and Gabe's skin had been so richly golden in that light . . .

Wearily, Sara slumped down in a chair and rubbed her shoulders. When love is over, the pain should die. But love was not so kind, she thought bleakly. It just throbbed on and on long after the physical substance of it was extracted. Her father had once given her a workable philosophy: *go have your cry, Sara, then get on with it*. She'd already had her cry, and it was time to—

"Get on with it," Sara whispered, dropping her face into her hands. That last part required a great deal of effort at times.

She showered and slipped into a pale green kimono, then cleaned the already spotless apartment. Some of Billie's clutter would have been supremely welcome, she thought, gazing around the sterile room. Sara sorely missed the warm, lovely woman, and that irrepressible good humor that could always lift her heart.

As if a magic genie was responsive to her wishes, the door flew open and a squealing, fur-wrapped blond burst into the room. Effusive cries of joy mounted to fever pitch as the two friends greeted each other. Billie launched her barrage of questions long before Sara was finished hugging her.

Laughing, Sara answered them, drolly extolling the virtues of her second job. Billie was aghast, but there were more pressing matters. She wagged a finger in Sara's face and accused, "Sara Tracey, how could you not tell me how absolutely gorgeous your Gabe is! My goodness, he's a living doll—and so sexy! I swear if I hadn't—"

"Wait a minute—you saw Gabe?" Sara exclaimed.

"Oh yes! He took me to dinner—"

"Gabe Fielding took you to dinner?"

"He certainly did! And I tell you, Sara, he's absolutely fabulous! Had he so much as crooked a finger, I'd have thrown myself into his arms!" Billie declared. "And on my honeymoon at that!"

"Yes, he is rather hard on a lady's virtue," Sara dazedly agreed. "Billie, Billie, wait—slow down a minute, will you? Just how on earth did you come to meet Gabe, let alone have dinner with him!"

"Well, Sara, it was the craziest thing," Billie confided. "Glen and I were staying at the Kahala Hilton—in Honolulu—and I was in the lobby when I heard a Gabe Fielding being paged. Well of course I immediately began looking around to see if it was your

Gabe, and it was—I knew it from your description! So I hurried right over and introduced myself as your friend, and he knew instantly who I was!"

"And then?" Sara croaked.

"And then he invited me to dinner, and said it was too fantastic just to pass by like strangers. Glen had a dreary business dinner scheduled for that night and I much preferred Gabe's invitation, so I said yes, of course!"

"I see. What did you talk about, Billie?" Sara asked quietly.

"Oh, scads of things! I think he's utterly adorable and how you walked away from him, I'll never never know! But he said you did, that you were just friends. I told him I didn't doubt that for a minute!" Billie merrily confessed.

"Thanks, I appreciate that," said Sara dryly. "But you didn't get personal, Billie? About me, I mean?"

"Heavens, no! Mostly we talked about me. He was so interested in my life and how I met you and all—and Glen joined us shortly after dinner and just took over the conversation. Jealous, I guess," Billie murmured complacently. Remembering she still had on her coat, she pitched the beautiful garment in the direction of the couch, then sat down and crossed her sleek legs.

Eyeing that deep, honeyed tan, Sara felt as pallid as a slug in comparison. She took the other chair and clasped Billie's hand in a squeeze of love. "You didn't, by any chance, mention Glen's loan, or its purpose?" she anxiously inquired.

Billie looked shocked. "Of course not, Sara! Didn't I promise to keep it a deep, dark secret? Although I simply cannot comprehend why you felt compelled to do such a thing—why, Gabe's a lovely man! So warm and friendly—you could tell right off he's not a stingy person!"

"It's a personal matter, Billie. But in case I didn't thank you properly for attending it, thank you, love. You'll never know how much it meant to me to know I'll get that jewelry back. Look, I've got over a hundred and fifty dollars already; that's why the other job, of course," Sara exulted. She got the canister and emptied it on the table. "I'll pay Glen back in no time, you'll see," she assured.

Billie touched a dainty finger to the crumpled heap of bills. "Oh, fiddlesticks, Sara!" she said irritably. "To be honest, I forgot all about it. On one's honeymoon, one does tend to forget things. Anyway, Glen has loads of money, and certainly doesn't need your four hundred dollars! I'll bring your jewelry next time I come."

"No, Billie," Sara said gently. She scooped up the money, smiling at Billie's grimace. "It's an honorable debt, a very fine thing that Glen did, and I appreciate it, honey, but this is between your husband and me. Besides, I can afford it. Alex gave me a very nice raise when we got back—just out of the blue! So everything's going fine for me . . ."

Her voice deepened. "Billie, how did he look—what was he wearing?" Coloring, Sara quickly turned her face—what a stupid question! And yet, she listened hungrily to Billie's response.

"As I said, he looked wonderful—relaxed, tanned, a teasing sort of man, and the most wonderful company! I really enjoyed talking to him, and so did Glen. And he was wearing . . . well, a gray suit and blue linen shirt when we had dinner. He looks marvelous in his clothes—I told him he should take up modeling!" she

171

chattered artlessly. "Oh, on the second day, I saw him and a fabulous looking blond in the lobby. I only caught a glimpse of them, but she looked like a whipped cream confection, all white and gold—" Billie faltered as Sara abruptly turned away.

"Yes, I know. Well listen, I've got exactly ten minutes to get into that snazzy uniform and hie myself down to Broyhill's! I hate to break this off. Oh, Billie, it's so good to see you, so good! Where are you living? And are you back for good, or is this merely a respite from honeymooning?"

Sara followed her friend to the door with her own belated questions. Considerably more subdued, Billie assured her that she was back for good, living in Glen's penthouse apartment, and they must get together very soon.

"I've still got tons of things to tell you—tonight hardly made a dent!" she accused. She paused in the open door for another hug. "Sara, did you walk away from it? Intact, I mean?" she asked softly. "Maybe I've been just a little dense about—about things, and if so, I'm sorry, darling."

Searching brown eyes met steady blue ones. Why mar Billie's happiness? "Yes, Billie, I walked away from it . . . more or less intact," Sara said.

She had precious little time to waste once Billie flew out the door. As she got into her uniform, Sara had to chuckle at the image of Billie's moment of recognition. Knowing her friend's impetuous spirit, Gabe must have thought a tornado struck him! She grabbed her sweater and raced down the stairs, trying to cope with the bitter realization that Billie's news had torn scabs off still-tender sores. Moneta was with him in Honolulu. The agonizing thought pulsed with every beat of her heart.

The next two days provided a severe test of Sara's temper. Alex was surly and uncommunicative, and everything she did was wrong. Knowing that he had embarked on one of his marathon writing sessions, she held her tongue, but her own depression was ill-equipped to deal with his black mood.

Along towards noon, he stomped in and tossed a heavily embossed invitation on her desk. "Black tie, Friday night at the Sherry-Netherland," he muttered. His eyebrows knit together in a challenging frown. "You are free, aren't you?" Alex asked, watching her closely.

"Me?" Sara asked, surprised.

"Yes, you. Read the invitation—your name's right on there, isn't it?" he growled. "Blast, who made this coffee? Tastes like burned noodles!"

Sara didn't remind him that he had made it. "I'll make another pot . . . Alex, I'm sorry, but I'm not free that night," she said very gently.

"Then you'll just have to get free, won't you," Alex acidly returned.

Sara was well enough acquainted with Alex's views to know he would heartily resent her moonlighting. Had he found her out? "I'll try, Alex."

"You'll do more than try—this is business. I'm the guest speaker, damn it! Why the devil did you let me get roped into this? If there's anything in the world I don't need . . ." Giving her the look of a much put upon man, he slouched back to his study.

Sara waited until the door closed behind him before daring to laugh. If there was anything Alex Brandt loved more than being asked to speak to a group—any group—she couldn't name it! But she did have a nasty little complication to unravel; how to get herself free. She had not worked at the café long enough to demand a night off for anything other than illness, and unfortunately, she was in perfect health.

Well, Alex had priority. If she had to get fired, better the restaurant job. Meantime, the banquet was only two days away, and as far as she knew, he hadn't even begun to write a speech. How long had he known about this? Probably weeks, she thought with resignation. He did have a tendency to procrastinate.

A few minutes later, her name reverberated through the apartment, and Sara picked up her steno pad and hastened to the study.

By six that evening, they had a reasonable facsimile of a speech, and she had a dull headache. Just before she left the office, Alex suddenly gave her his sweet, sheepish smile, and she forgave him everything from three years back. A person could get a lot further in this world if they didn't have a bowl of mush for a heart, Sara thought whimsically.

"Sara?"

She turned at the door. "Yes, sir?"

"Don't suppose you'd want to have dinner with an old grouch?"

He suddenly looked a very lonely man, standing there with his hands jammed in his pockets, and Sara wondered—not for the first time—if he too had left a part of himself on the island. "Thank you, but I have a prior engagement. I really wish I didn't, Alex. Goodnight, and get some sleep, hum?" she gently urged.

An hour later, when Sara opened the door of her own apartment, a heavenly wave of fragrance flowed out to greet her. Stunned, she dropped her bag of groceries on the couch and delightedly approached the glorious extravaganza practically covering the coffee-table. It was the most magnificent arrangement of spring flowers: tulips, jonquils, hyacinths, great purple sheaths of lilacs, tiny pink roses and dancing babies' breath, iris like dainty cream and blue butterflies three to a stem, the tiniest of ferns . . .

"Lovely!" she breathed rapturously. From whom? There was no card—she searched frantically, but there was none. "Oh, of course—from Billie!" she exclaimed. Billie could afford such extravagant gestures now, and it was right up her alley. Rushing to the telephone, Sara dialed with shaking fingers. The singsong voice of Glen's housekeeper informed her that Mr. and Mrs. Glen had left for San Francisco that afternoon and would return in three days. Disappointed, Sara thanked him and hung up.

She sat awhile and enjoyed the exquisite flowers. How lovely that someone thought enough of her to make a gesture like that. If only she could tell Billie how very much it meant to her! Inexpressibly warmed by such thoughtfulness, Sara put away her groceries, then went to the bedroom to change clothes. From a chic gabardine blazer and skirt to a blue cotton uniform, she thought, one extreme to another. Clad for the moment in her lacy bra and panties, Sara stilled, remembering how Gabe had looked at her in that scanty bikini, his eyes deep green and gleaming as he touched her, kissed her, whispered her name.

A physical wave of longing shuddered through her. Swiftly she turned from the mirror and snatched up the uniform, putting it on with fumbling haste to cover her body, to blot out memories.

What was he doing, right now, this very minute? The need to know was shocking in its intensity. She drew a shaky breath and finished buttoning up. She had not dated since returning to New York, and the reason for it was extremely disturbing.

Weighing the men she knew against Gabe, she felt again the fear which haunted thoughts of the future. What if she never found anyone who measured up?

Thank heavens she had little time to think about all the things which crouched at the back of her mind, Sara grumbled—she'd be a mental case! She grabbed her purse and flew out the door, and by the time she stumbled back through it, her face was gray with exhaustion. Three hours later the alarm went off, and she was back on her treadmill and who had time to think of anything save getting through this day!

Alex was restless and grumpy and she bit her cheek a time or two, but against all odds, they managed to part friends at the end of the day.

"Remember, meet me in the hotel lobby no later than seven thirty," he reminded as she left the office.

"Yes, seven thirty. And don't forget your speech. Maybe I'd better take the spare copy, just in case," Sara decided. Alex gave her a disgusted look at this lack of trust, but she took it anyway.

She spared time to water her flowers before bathing and dressing for tonight's affair. Billie possessed so many clothes, she hadn't bothered taking half of them, and Sara had half a dozen chic gowns to choose from. The one she selected was a luscious shade of raspberry pink crepe de chine, strapless, exquisitely simple and flattering. Once dressed and coiffed, she gave herself critical assessment, but only for Alex's sake; there was no real pleasure in her striking appearance.

She ought to be thrilled by the honor of accompanying her famous boss to this affair, but in truth, she'd just as soon put on a nightgown and curl up with a book. She was tired and depressed and uncertain of her ability to meet tonight's demands.

Unable to get a cab at once, she was also fifteen minutes late, and Alex was pacing. However, his mood had taken a remarkable turn for the better. Eyeing the broad grin on his face, Sara wondered at his inordinate upswing. Alex caught her quizzical look and grinned even wider.

"I talked with Janet tonight. She's coming to town next week," he leaned close to whisper. "She showed me Houston, now I'll show her New York—it's only fair," he gravely assured.

"Oh, Alex, that's wonderful! How long will she be staying?"

"Well, she wants to see New York, and as you know, there's an awful lot of New York to see!" he chortled.

"An awful lot—why, it could take weeks," Sara joyously agreed.

His speech was well received, especially when he began deviating from the script in one of his wild, woolly, slightly risqué tangents. Even Sara was convulsed at his wit. Afterwards there was dancing, but she declined all offers; to earn this time off, she had worked five hours overtime the night before at the café in a swap with one of the other waitresses, and the rest of the evening was simply to be gotten through. Standing aside, listening to conversation which thankfully excluded her, she forced herself to keep her drooping head erect as she idly scanned the crowd.

Like an electric prod, the shock of seeing a familiar dark head snapped her to rigid attention. His back was turned—it wasn't him—it couldn't be him! Hot, cold, unable to draw a decent breath, Sara waited in an agony of suspense for the man to turn.

And then he did. Relaxed and assured in a cream jersey turtleneck under a rich chocolate brown jacket, Gabe made all the men in their formal attire look stuffy and overdressed.

A liquid gush of joy raced through her like unfurling banners. Greedily she drank in the curving mouth, the jade green eyes, the grace of his slim-hipped figure. As he came toward her, Sara struggled with outrageous happiness. She had to get hold of her giddy self, find a semblance of composure—

"Hello, Sara." Gabe smiled politely.

"Gabe. This is a surprise . . ." Feeling utterly spent, Sara cast about for something else to say but her mind was a blank. Just then Alex joined them. His pleased surprise at seeing Gabe seemed genuine; Sara's instant suspicion shamed her as she listened to his delighted greeting, yet she intuitively sensed that Gabe's presence at this affair was not coincidental.

When Gabe smoothly halted conversation to request a dance, she could only nod. The shock of seeing him was still a wild singing in her heart, impossible to calm, impractical to reveal. Only by feigning bored indifference could she get through this. Placing a hand lightly on his shoulder, she looked up at him and received another shock. His face was set in a bland, impersonal mask which mocked her feeble efforts. She might have been dancing with a stranger for all the warmth in his manner.

"You look thinner, even peaked," he dispassionately observed.

"I've lost a few pounds. What are you doing here?" she asked coldly.

"I had business here, both professional and personal." He shrugged, letting his gaze drift beyond her.

"I've accomplished the former, but the latter may require more finesse than I possess." An ironic smile curved his mouth as he glanced at her again.

"As usual, I don't understand," she said. She was back to playing a part again, she despaired.

"It's very simple, Sara. When you left the island, you took something of mine. Naturally I would like it returned."

Sara stopped dead, her eyes wide as saucers at this astounding accusation. "W-what are you talking about? I took nothing of yours!"

"Lower your voice," Gabe said sharply. "We can't discuss it here. Shall we leave now?"

"Leave?" she echoed.

"Yes—unless you'd rather drag Alex into it?"

"Oh no! No, I—Gabe, you can't be serious!" she said with an incredulous little laugh.

"Unfortunately, I'm deadly serious," he coldly informed her.

Sara shook her head as if to clear it. This was crazy—he couldn't be serious! When she looked up, an implacable mask confronted her. "But what—you said I took something—what?" she stammered.

An eyebrow slanted. "This is hardly the place to discuss a theft, Sara. Now I suggest we get out of here and settle this. I'm leaving for Mexico in an hour and I don't have time to waste," he said impatiently. The dance had ended, but Sara simply stood in place, staring at him. "Well?" he prodded. Too confused to resist, she nodded.

"You wait here, I'll tell Alex we're leaving," Gabe ordered.

Dumbly Sara obeyed. Where were they going? Did he really think she was a thief? She didn't know what to think! He was back and with her evening bag and wrap. As he placed it around her shoulders, his eyes dropped to the swelling curve of her upper breasts, translucent against the glowing gown. His fingertips glided down her neck. She jerked aside.

"Let's go, Sara," he said huskily.

Dazedly she nodded. All kaleidoscopic thoughts and surging eagerness, her sway of slender hips preceded him to the limousine waiting at the curb.

"All right, let's go," Gabe tersely told the chauffeur. He closed the glass partition, and turned to Sara, who sat in the far corner of the seat.

"Did you like the flowers?" he asked pleasantly.

"The flowers . . . were from you?"

"Yes."

Driven to distraction by his nearness, Sara clenched her fists and tried to think. "All right, let's get to it, Gabe. What's this all about?" she asked resignedly.

Her heart gave a convulsive leap as he reached for her. "Come here, Sara—oh, darling, come here!" he said fiercely. Beyond astonishment, she mindlessly turned to him, and a heartbeat later, she was being kissed with passionate hunger. "Oh, Sara, I missed you," Gabe groaned.

Sara was rendered incapable of speech or movement, other than the ones her hands were making through his thick, silky hair, roaming in delighted abandon as his mouth came down on hers again with thrilling urgency. There was a man in the front seat, she dimly remembered, and Gabe was holding her molded against him, straightening his legs to meet her thighs in intimate communion, kissing with the starved need of newly reunited lovers, and it was all utterly unreal. She felt her hair tumbling down, his hands tangling in it, his deep groan of pleasure on her lips. The aroused excitement of his body was implicit in his voice as he whispered her name again and again.

Sara struggled weakly against engulfing rapture. He touched and held and kissed her as if discovering some rare and wonderful thing, and his touch was fire, his mouth a burning brand upon her skin. "Oh, Sara, I want you, I need you," he said in a deep, hurting groan. Her world careened, then stabilized with stunning rapidity as his words sunk in. His obsession—not her, his hateful obsession! No theft—just a trick—her thoughts funneled into fury and outrage. She squirmed wildly, pummeling his shoulders, hating him, loving him and mad enough to slap him at the slightest provocation.

"You tricked me—let me go!" she cried wildly.

He kissed her. "No, Sara, never again. We're getting married tonight, tomorrow at the latest. I have a plane waiting at LaGuardia; we're going to Mexico and then to the island. And after a suitable time, we'll fly to France to meet my parents. They'll love you," he assured.

Sara sagged bonelessly against the seat.

"You're insane," she said after a time.

"I love you, Sara," Gabe softly replied.

There was a very long silence. Distractedly Sara glanced out the window—they really were on their way to the airport! I've lost my mind, she thought tiredly. She looked at the man beside her, infinitely loved and desired, and distrusted. He had been with Moneta in Honolulu only last week, and now he was here, saying he loved her. She began to cry soundlessly.

"Sara?" he prompted.

"What game are you playing now, Gabe?" she asked bitterly.

"Oh, love, no games!" He touched her face and found the tears. "Don't cry, darling, please don't cry," he said huskily.

His duplicity was unbearable! "Oh stop it—just stop it! I'm too tired for this. I worked until five this morning and I'm tired!" she wailed.

"Why did you work until five this morning?" he asked, clearly surprised.

"Because of you, that's why! Because I sold my mother's jewelry to pay back your money—because now I owe another man four hundred dollars!" she screamed in a jumble of pain and outrage.

"Sara," Gabe sighed deeply. He pillowed her wet face in his shoulder and dropped his own to her fragrant mass of hair. "I'm sorry, baby, but I had to take a chance. Sara, it was my heart you took from the island. I knew I loved you after I made that idiotic proposal of marriage and you told me so clearly what a fool I was. But I learned too late—you said you despised Robert Fielding—and I saw the way you looked at me . . ." Sara heard his sigh. "I knew I'd ruined it for us, so I let you go."

Wanting desperately to believe him, she raised her face. "Yes, you let me go! And a month later you suddenly decided to . . . why *did* you decide to?"

"If a man can't find a reason to get up in the morning, he's got to take a chance, even if he's quite certain the lady in question despises him."

Instantly responsive to his bleak tone, Sara reached up and fiercely kissed him. "I love you, you idiot! I loved you when you were Gabe and I loved you when you were Robert—I've always loved you! How could you be so dense, so stupid, so utterly blind about a thing like that!"

"Sara . . . my lovely little Sara . . ."

Later, she asked softly, "Moneta?"

"Moneta? What about her?" he blankly returned.

"You were with her that last night—"

"Sara, that was an act of sheer defiance, as were all the other times I saw her," Gabe said roughly. "You had me so mixed up and hurt, I couldn't think straight, a rather common phenomenon when I'm around you. I cared nothing for Moneta—I broke our engagement because I realized that."

"You broke the engagement?"

"Yes, honey, I did the leaving. But Moneta's family are old friends, and I respect them, so I just let her explain it as she liked."

"Billie told me she'd met you," Sara pursued the subject in a roundabout way. "What did she tell you about me?"

"Actually very little. Your charming friend has a marvelous talent for talking nonstop and saying nothing. But just seeing her, listening to the sound of your name . . . that's when I decided I had to try."

"She thought Moneta was too beautiful to be real," Sara remarked.

Gabe sat back in tired defeat. "I see. Moneta's presence in Honolulu was sheer coincidence, at least on my part. We exchanged a few words in the lobby, and that was it."

"I'm sorry, Gabe, I didn't mean to cross-examine you, but I knew you were with her in Honolulu just last week, and now you're here with me, saying you love me—I just don't want to get hurt again."

Gabe cupped her face in his two big hands, his voice ragged. "Sara, I'm sorry, so very sorry for all the times I hurt you, deliberately or otherwise. And some of it *was* deliberate, like that incident with Alana. Let me tell you why that happened, why I behaved so brutally—"

"I know why. Skeet told me. You don't have to explain it, darling," Sara softly interrupted.

"Skeet told you? Then I owe him one. But it requires further explanation, honey. Because it wasn't just that. Alana was just an excuse to strike out at you. Sara, all those things I said about love and marriage and women, I really believed them, and when the time came, I intended to select a wife the same way I'd select a horse, with *logic,* not feeling." His voice deepened. "It was sheer accident that I saw you at the pool that day. I freely admit I shouldn't have watched, but I did. You were so lovely, so happy, and yet, Sara, from the first moment I met you, I was angry at you! You shook me in a way no one's ever done—oh, love, you would say something in that lofty, innocent way that delights me so, and I would feel it so sharply I had to react with sarcasm or a cynical remark, just to defend myself against your appeal. And then your pretty face would cloud with that wounded look you get and I would despise myself and get even madder at you!"

He sighed deeply. "When I was off the island, I couldn't think of anything but coming back; when I was there, I was torn between wanting to see you and hating this weakness for an impertinent little woman who didn't seem to care if I went or stayed. By the time the incident with Alana happened, I felt like a boiling pot with the lid clamped on too tight. And when you came riding in on Alana, it was all I needed to blow the lid off and release all that resentment and tension—because I could justify it. Alana was obviously in distress and I had a reason to explode. And then you looked at me as if I'd slapped you and I . . . Oh, Sara, I felt savage with self-disgust, shame, anger, the same vicious cycle all over again. And when I came to see you that night, you were so cold and hurt, I reacted in the usual stupid fashion."

He laughed, rawly. "I went up there and searched until I found your hat lying in a mudhole. I took it to Houston, told them to repair it or else have a madman on their hands! Needless to say, I was still feeling savage. Sara, there was never a time that you could not have asked me for anything under the sun and I would have given it. That's why I got so wild when you sent me that check; it pleased me so much to give you those clothes that weekend in Houston."

"You didn't cash that check, did you?" Sara accused.

"No, of course not. In fact, I've been thinking of having it framed, sort of a constant reminder of the fact that I have a very proud, highminded wife . . . that is, if I have that wife. Sara, will you marry me? For love and mutual respect and until death do us part?"

"If you're quite sure that's what you want, Gabe," she said quietly. Remembering his other proposal, she added in a colder tone, "Because that's exactly what you'd be getting—"

"Because that's exactly what I want. Just you, and for always. Marry me?"

It was rather like being hit with an avalanche of joy! She looked up at him, an impish gleam in her eyes. "Well, I suppose it can be arranged. Of course, you'll have to sign some sort of waiver—I have no intention of giving you half the Tracey assets," she said with lilting impudence. "And we'll have to sit down together and draw up a bill of rights—"

Gabe's joyous burst of laughter hushed her mischief.

185

"Oh, Sara, my sweet Sara! Do you know how near to crazy you drove me?" he asked incredulously. "Trying to figure you out—does she or doesn't she, will she or won't she—what the devil is she! And just when I thought I had it figured out, you'd come up with a whole new angle and start hitting me again!"

Sara began giggling all over his joyous indignation. "I'm so sorry, Gabe. I apologize for hitting you, I apologize for confusing you, I apologize for driving you crazy—and if that doesn't do it—"

"Sara Lynne Tracey, I love you!" Gabe roared wildly.

"And I love you, Robert Gabriel Fielding," she whispered.

"Even though I've got a terrible temper and I'm the most obnoxious, arrogant, absolutely impossible man you've ever met?" he asked hopefully.

"Even so. But I'll reform you. . . . I'll have my work cut out for me, I suspect!" Trustingly Sara nestled in his arms and surrendered fully to the certainty of his love. They kissed, tenderly, playfully, joyously, passionately, a long interval of intimacy which healed all wounds. A lucid thought managed to occur to her as they entered the airport. Twisting in the arms which had no intention of letting her go, she looked up at him with rounding eyes.

"Gabe, I can't possibly just up and leave like this! There's Alex—"

"I informed Alex of my intentions. He wished me luck," Gabe drawled.

"But I don't even have a toothbrush—"

"I own chains of drugstores."

"Well—well, not even a change of clothes—"

"You won't need any, not for weeks."

"Not even a nightgown, Gabe," she joyously protested.

"And certainly not a nightgown."

"But, Gabe—"

"Hush," said Gabe, and hushed her in his own inimitable way.

IT'S YOUR OWN SPECIAL TIME

Contemporary romances for today's women.
Each month, six very special love stories will be yours
from SILHOUETTE. Look for them wherever books are sold
or order now from the coupon below.

$1.50 each

☐ 5 Goforth	☐ 28 Hampson	☐ 54 Beckman	☐ 83 Halston
☐ 6 Stanford	☐ 29 Wildman	☐ 55 LaDame	☐ 84 Vitek
☐ 7 Lewis	☐ 30 Dixon	☐ 56 Trent	☐ 85 John
☐ 8 Beckman	☐ 32 Michaels	☐ 57 John	☐ 86 Adams
☐ 9 Wilson	☐ 33 Vitek	☐ 58 Stanford	☐ 87 Michaels
☐ 10 Caine	☐ 34 John	☐ 59 Vernon	☐ 88 Stanford
☐ 11 Vernon	☐ 35 Stanford	☐ 60 Hill	☐ 89 James
☐ 17 John	☐ 38 Browning	☐ 61 Michaels	☐ 90 Major
☐ 19 Thornton	☐ 39 Sinclair	☐ 62 Halston	☐ 92 McKay
☐ 20 Fulford	☐ 46 Stanford	☐ 63 Brent	☐ 93 Browning
☐ 22 Stephens	☐ 47 Vitek	☐ 71 Ripy	☐ 94 Hampson
☐ 23 Edwards	☐ 48 Wildman	☐ 73 Browning	☐ 95 Wisdom
☐ 24 Healy	☐ 49 Wisdom	☐ 76 Hardy	☐ 96 Beckman
☐ 25 Stanford	☐ 50 Scott	☐ 78 Oliver	☐ 97 Clay
☐ 26 Hastings	☐ 52 Hampson	☐ 81 Roberts	☐ 98 St. George
☐ 27 Hampson	☐ 53 Browning	☐ 82 Dailey	☐ 99 Camp

$1.75 each

☐ 100 Stanford	☐ 110 Trent	☐ 120 Carroll	☐ 130 Hardy
☐ 101 Hardy	☐ 111 South	☐ 121 Langan	☐ 131 Stanford
☐ 102 Hastings	☐ 112 Stanford	☐ 122 Scofield	☐ 132 Wisdom
☐ 103 Cork	☐ 113 Browning	☐ 123 Sinclair	☐ 133 Rowe
☐ 104 Vitek	☐ 114 Michaels	☐ 124 Beckman	☐ 134 Charles
☐ 105 Eden	☐ 115 John	☐ 125 Bright	☐ 135 Logan
☐ 106 Dailey	☐ 116 Lindley	☐ 126 St. George	☐ 136 Hampson
☐ 107 Bright	☐ 117 Scott	☐ 127 Roberts	☐ 137 Hunter
☐ 108 Hampson	☐ 118 Dailey	☐ 128 Hampson	☐ 138 Wilson
☐ 109 Vernon	☐ 119 Hampson	☐ 129 Converse	☐ 139 Vitek

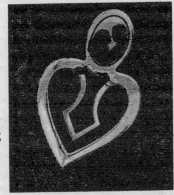

Silhouette **Romance**

15-Day Free Trial Offer
6 Silhouette Romances

6 Silhouette Romances, free for 15 days! We'll send you 6 new Silhouette Romances to keep for 15 days, absolutely free! If you decide not to keep them, send them back to us. You pay nothing.

Free Home Delivery. But if you enjoy them as much as we think you will, keep them by paying the invoice enclosed with your free trial shipment. We'll pay all shipping and handling charges. You get the convenience of Home Delivery and we pay the postage and handling charge each month.

Don't miss a copy. The Silhouette Book Club is the way to make sure you'll be able to receive every new romance we publish before they're sold out. There is no minimum number of books to buy and you can cancel at any time.

This offer expires November 30, 1983